CONNECTIONS

CONNECTIONS

A COLLECTION OF SHORT STORIES
EDITED BY FUZZY FLAMINGO

First published in 2021 by Fuzzy Flamingo
www.fuzzyflamingo.co.uk

© 2021 Jen Parker

ISBN: 978-1-8384388-2-1

Cover design and typesetting: Fuzzy Flamingo
www.fuzzyflamingo.co.uk

For all those affected by the pandemic

CONTENTS

CONNECTIONS

FOREWORD

By Jen Parker, Fuzzy Flamingo

This second collection of short stories has been written by a community of writers ranging from traditionally published authors through to self-published authors and first timers. I am delighted that some of the authors from my first volume, *Escape Reality*, wanted to join in with this second project, and it is a joy to see their writing develop.

The first project started at the beginning of the first lockdown back in March 2020. When national lockdown began, I'd already been shielding and was feeling the stress creep in with balancing my work and having my girls, Lily and Amber, at home full time needing my attention. I have always found reading and writing therapeutic, feeling able to get lost in good books and escaping the pressures of life for a while. I wanted to share that and so put a call-out on social media for authors and would-be authors to come together and write short stories to take their minds off what was happening in the real world.

The first book was a success, getting to number two

in the Amazon best-seller charts, becoming an Amazon number one 'hot new release' and receiving great reviews. But more than that, the authors were doing something for themselves, they really enjoyed the project and built friendships within the private author group on Facebook.

So, when some of the authors asked me if there would be the opportunity to do it again with a second collection, how could I say no? When I launched the second short story project, I got a great response from the authors in volume one, as well as new authors wanting to join in. Shortly after the private author group was set up on Facebook, though, we went into another national lockdown. All of a sudden, many of the authors were facing additional challenges with home-schooling again (I was extremely grateful that nurseries stayed open, so my childcare could remain in place) and juggling new work pressures. This makes it even more rewarding for me that they have still thrown themselves into their writing and got so much from it.

I would like to say a huge thank you to all of the authors taking part, as well as everyone who has supported the short story collection projects. Every social media post, like, comment, share, means the world to me, as it helps me on my mission to show the world how powerful and therapeutic reading and writing can be. Thank you to the reviewers, including Tania Taylor who is quoted on the back cover. Thanks also to the two wonderful authors in this collection who did the proofreading for me, Emma Davies and Laura Bland. And finally, thank you to Gemma Barder, the professional author who took time out to offer support, inspiration and feedback to her co-authors in this collection. Your advice has been invaluable.

I'd love to hear what you think of the book, so please do leave a review on Amazon, or contact me via my website: www.fuzzyflamingo.co.uk

If you would like to join a community of book lovers, whether you are a writer or a reader (or even if you are wanting to get inspired to do either) then join in on Facebook:
https://www.facebook.com/groups/ fuzzyflamingobooklovers

FOR THE LOVE OF BOOKS

Gemma Barder

It had started well. He was tall (which is a bonus) and friendly. He held the door of the café open for me to walk through, which shows good manners. He asked if I had any trouble finding the place; I hadn't. I didn't want to tell him that I had actually been there lots of times before. He seemed to think he'd discovered it. It was one of those places that people love to tell other people about. Trendy, but not unwelcoming. Good coffee, but not too pricey. Comfy seats and plenty of nooks to curl up in. The owners had got it just right.

Adam had managed to reserve a table in a quiet corner and we started the usual chat of two people who had only ever met online. We talked about the weather and whether or not to get food as well as a coffee, but in reality, we were sizing up how accurately our profile pictures matched our real, unfiltered faces.

To be fair to Adam, he looked pretty much as I expected him to. Perhaps his hair was a little thinner on top, but that didn't matter. We ordered and, as I passed my menu back to the young waiter with floppy hair and thick glasses, I prepared myself for the inevitable. The preamble was over and now it was time to talk. Properly talk. Not the weather, not traffic. Proper stuff. We covered jobs and family in record time. He seemed interested in me (florist, one sister, brother-in-law, both of them accountants, one dog) and I was interested in him (cameraman, two brothers, three dogs at home with his mum and dad).

Remember I said it started well? That was probably misleading. It middled well, too. We'd shaken off the awkwardness of a first date and the conversation flowed happily and easily. Food done with; it was time to talk pastimes. This could have been the moment Adam revealed he spent his weekends conducting civil war re-enactments or morris dancing. The truth was more conventional (dare I say boring?): cycling, running, box sets on Netflix.

'I like to read,' I said.

I said it like it was simply a hobby. A few paragraphs before bed. I was sensible enough to ease him into it. The truth being far greater. Far more important. He was gracious enough to ask what I liked to read, though I suspect it was more out of politeness than interest. The young waiter reappeared with two excellent coffees, which gave me time to breathe.

How to answer a question like that? What *did* I like to read? Anything, everything. From Daniel Defoe to Mills and Boon. Chaucer to Mantel. Books were everything. They were my passion, my lifeblood. How could I explain to this man I had only just met, the feeling of holding an unread book in my hands? The endless possibilities that lay beneath the cover. The journey of emotions it could lead me on. How could I explain the comfort that a pile of unread books on my nightstand could give? Far greater than any relationship I had ever known. The knowledge that no matter what happened in the world, those books, those words, those stories would remain. Steadfast and waiting. Patient and loyal.

I gave a standard reply as I stirred in a tiny sachet of brown sugar, destroying the waiter's latte art. This and that, classics, some modern fiction. He nodded enthusiastically.

And here, I'm afraid, is where the possibility that real life offers failed to match the possibility of an unread book. Looking back, I shouldn't have asked. I know from experience how well this question goes. But Adam seemed kind. His manners were impeccable. Perhaps today, this afternoon, eating good food and good coffee in a nice café with steamed up windows and rain falling outside. Perhaps the answer would be the right one.

'Do you read much?' I asked.

Adam smiled and replaced his cup onto its saucer. He looked me straight in the eye, not knowing the weight of importance his answer held. Time stood still. I held my breath.

'Not really, I prefer to be outdoors,' he replied.

★

I ran my fingers over the spines of my favourite shelf of books; well-thumbed favourites; cloth-bound classics;

mottled Penguin paperbacks found in charity shops; and looked back at my afternoon.

I managed to get through the rest of the date with dignity. Like eating a piece of dry cake a friend has offered you. Smiling, but not really enjoying yourself.

Flopping onto the sofa, I reached for my current book – a meandering post-war tale of a young man's journey along the north-west coast. I cracked the spine and found my place. My phone was flicked onto silent and placed deliberately screen down. I needed at least an hour for my mind to wander before I could tell the well-worn tale of: 'Nice chap, not for me.'

The evening light began to fade and my eyes grew tired. I folded the corner of my page (no amount of gifted bookmarks could entice me to use one) and breathed deeply. I flipped the screen of my phone to see three messages. One from Mum and one from a friend, both asking how my lunch had gone. The last was from my sister.

'Angus took on a new client today. He owns a bookshop.'

★★★

Gemma has worked in publishing for over eighteen years, first in magazines, then becoming an author of children's books. She has adapted classics for children, including Austen and Tolstoy, as well as writing picture books and activity books. As well as this, she co-publishes a quarterly magazine for the Harborough area. Gemma was thrilled to be able to help out in the creation of *Connections*, giving guidance to the writers involved, as well as contributing her own story. You can find more about Gemma here:

scruffygiraffe.com/books

THE PEBBLES

Laura Bland

I stared blankly at the coloured pebbles in front of me, my gaze went straight through them. I no longer saw the browns and oranges, the whites and blues. I no longer saw the perfectly rounded edges and smooth surfaces. All I saw was a desperate rage. A rage that I had been pushing down, deep down inside of me as far as it could go for years, but which was threatening to spill out. I could feel it rise up, right behind my eyes like a building pressure, it was ready to spill over and consume me.

I stayed where I was, motionless and staring. I focused my thoughts on my breathing to bring back some calm and gradually I began to see the pebbles again. I sought out my favourite ones, one a burnt red somehow forged over time into the shape of a love heart, another almost purple in hue, so flat and smooth that I longed to see what it felt like. The rage started to withdraw; I began to stamp it back down where it belonged. Pushing my feelings aside once again, I let out a resigned sigh; it was just another day, another mood swing, another jump in his unpredictable nature.

I should have been used to it by now but, every time, it caught me off guard. The change in him was so fast it was like the flick of a switch yet so unpredictable.

I took another minute and one last deep breath before I moved. I slowly and deliberately stood up, my face was blank, devoid of any emotion, mirroring the way I felt in that moment; numb again. I knew it was a cycle I was bound to repeat for as long as I stayed, but I just didn't have the strength to do anything else. I knew that I should just leave, I knew it in my heart, but I just couldn't admit it out loud. I couldn't admit to being a failure, because that's what I was. There must have been something that I was doing to cause this and, until I could figure it out and stop whatever it was, I just needed to stay quiet, quiet and small.

★

I stared blankly at the coloured pebbles in front of me, my gaze went straight through them. I listened to the sounds of the water. So faint, but as long as I was still, I could hear its soothing motion. Its soft bubbling helped to calm me and bring me back down to myself. I waited for the rage to abate and slip away. For the pressure to recede, for the red to fade. I wasn't sure if it was my rage or his that scared me the most. I pushed it back down, deep down inside of me. When it was back below the surface, I would put my mask back on. I would arrange my features as best as I could not to draw any attention. I had tried to stay invisible, I had tried to do everything right; I hadn't tried hard enough, it seemed.

I stayed where I was, motionless and staring. I focused on

7

my breathing, using it to still my mind and my emotions. If I didn't gain control I was going to cry; the frustrations, the hurt, the anger, they were getting harder and harder to ignore and push aside. It felt like an actual pressure inside of me, like something needed to get out, to be let loose. I needed to gain control, to cry would be a sign of my own weakness and I refused to show that. I refused to let him see just how deeply his words and actions cut me down. I knew the tears would come later but for now I needed to keep them away.

I took another minute and one last deep breath before I moved. I let out a sigh and slowly stood up; I needed to be in a different space. I needed to breathe my own air and take some time to bury my emotions; I had to get them back inside the black box I had created. To allow myself to continue to feel – whether it was rage, anger, hurt, loneliness, or anything else – would be my undoing. I'd need to get the smile back in place soon, it would be down to me to make the first move towards peace. It didn't matter that I hadn't done anything wrong, or at least I didn't think I had. It didn't matter that I wasn't the one to fly off the handle and blow things out of all proportion. It would still be me that needed to fix things; the longer I left it, the harder it would be. I needed to get that smile back in place.

★

I stared blankly at the coloured pebbles in front of me, my gaze went straight through them. I no longer really saw the pebbles; their colours had been lost to me some time ago. At first when I had come here, I had found it comforting, soothing. The colours, the peace, the sounds of the water, I could lose myself to it and come back calmed and with a new perspective. Now, though, it took longer and longer for that to happen. My space, my safe zone, my little corner of peace no longer held me or helped me.

I stayed where I was, motionless and staring. I no longer came to the pebbles to find peace and be comforted. Now I just came to this spot because it was familiar. I knew I could lose myself, at least for a short time, and I needed that. I thought that if I could lose myself then maybe I could lose him as well; or at least that was what I hoped. It was futile, though; he was everywhere and nowhere all at once. My own rage was still present, I was angry at the world, I was angry at him, I was angry at myself. But what was the point? I just needed to calm and quiet the voices in my mind.

I took another minute and one last deep breath before I moved. I turned to him and smiled, a smile that never reached my eyes. A smile that hid a world of pain. I felt resigned to the pattern now. His flares in temper no longer surprised me but the silly little things that tipped him over the edge did. It was hard to predict what might set him off and that meant it was hard to minimise the risks. It was hard to stay out of the way. I could never quite manage to stay invisible for long enough. Whether it was days or it was weeks, the rage always came.

★

I stared blankly at the coloured pebbles in front of me, my gaze went straight through them. I knew from the moment he had got up that the day was going to be a rough one, I could see it in the way he moved. The way he didn't look at me when I had spoken and how he'd barely even grunted his replies at me. I wasn't even worthy of a real conversation now. I felt worthless. Why did I even bother? I didn't know if this was better or worse than before. I'd hoped I could stay out of the way. I'd hoped I could be small and invisible. I'd hoped… If I could just be invisible, then I might not trigger him. If I could just make myself as small as possible, then maybe I wouldn't tip him over the edge, maybe he would forget I was even there. Maybe. But here I was back in my spot, trying to shove it all back down and just switch my emotions back off.

I stayed where I was, motionless and staring. Waiting, though I'm not sure what for. I couldn't seem to find a smile inside of me. I delved as deep as I could but today it just wasn't there. There would be no slipping the mask back in place this day. This day there would just be avoidance, avoidance of everyone and everything. Maybe it was me? Maybe I was reading too much into it? Maybe I was just emotional and overreacting? Maybe I was the one that needed to gain control? I had tried my best, but it had been no good. I wasn't even sure what it had been this time. Had I left something out of place? Did I say the wrong thing? Was I just not good enough? Whatever it was, it had been enough to trigger his rage. He was shouting and slamming doors. I thought about answering back, about telling him how ridiculous he was being. But I didn't dare, I never did. Instead, I just went to my spot, my spot by the pebbles, and I sat. I sat for a long time, longer than normal.

I took another minute and one last deep breath before I

moved. I could feel the tears burning at the back of my eyes. I sat and held them back, but I wondered if I should just let them all out? Maybe that would make me feel better, maybe it would feel like some kind of release and I'd be able to move on and find a new emotion. Something more positive, something that would lift me out of my despair. I had curled my legs beneath me as I sat; I must have been there longer than I had realised, lost in the pebbles and my own mind. As I uncurled my legs and began to stretch them out in front of me, I was hit with the tingling sensation of pins and needles. It came at me in a wave and pushed me back down. I was in that place somewhere between pain and laughter, you know what I mean, you've been there. I was on the edge. It could go either way, but it didn't. I bit back the yelps of pain and I bit back the laughter. I knew better than to make even a single sound.

★

I was exhausted. Emotionally and mentally exhausted. I had cried a thousand tears a thousand times and there were probably a thousand more to come. I asked myself if I was okay. I asked myself if I could cope. I asked myself if I could carry on. It didn't really matter what the answer was. Did I even have a choice? This was my life and so I had to live it.

★

I stared blankly at the coloured pebbles in front of me, my gaze went straight through them. No matter how high the highs were, there was always a low just around the corner. It was never long before things came crashing back down and I was left wondering why. What had I done to deserve this? Was I being punished for some crime that I didn't even know I had committed? Maybe it was some terrible mistake, a nightmare I was soon to wake up from.

I stayed where I was, motionless and staring. My head felt heavy and my heart was sad. It was no longer rage that I felt, that emotion had died long ago. With it had gone all of my hopes and dreams, my passion and love. Now I was just resigned to what was happening. I knew it would never change. I was stuck in a cycle and it was going to keep on repeating. Unless...

I took another minute and one last deep breath before I moved. I stood up slowly, my movements deliberate and controlled. My face was devoid of any emotion. I was moving without effort or thought. My feet carried me forward, they were taking me towards freedom and away from everything that made me constantly doubt myself.

I kept on moving, I wasn't thinking anymore, I was just doing. I walked through the living room and out into the hallway. The floor was cold and hard beneath my feet, but I barely noticed. I had only one focus, one thing that I was moving towards. I wasn't thinking beyond the moment. I wasn't planning what might come next, I was just moving towards my destination. I stood in the doorway of the kitchen and stared at the chopping knives. I knew that any one of them would do the job, they were all razor sharp.

I had just one decision to make: him or me?

★★★

Laura is a mum of one based in Leicestershire with her daughter Callie and partner Leigh. She has loved to write from a very young age and has often used poetry and short story writing as a way to express and process her feelings. She now also offers her writing skills to other businesses and is often found writing blogs and other documents.
Laura is passionate about helping others to share their stories and has created multiple collaboration books herself.

You can find all of Laura's past books here:
Amazon.co.uk: Laura Bland: Books, Biography, Blogs, Audiobooks, Kindle
To find out how to work with Laura:
www.laurab-empoweredwords.com
info@laurab-empoweredwords.com

A TALE FROM THE FOREST

Samantha Latimer

In the woods, everything was still and calm and I heard the rustling of some tiny creature beneath, as it wended its way through the undergrowth, towards its family. Or its prey; I couldn't decide which. Maybe the tiny mammal was just having a little jaunt through the foliage, whiling away the time, with naught much to care about, or for. There was a slight murmuring sound, and if I stood still and didn't move, I could hear it, as it shifted through the unstirring air. That sound is the hum of the forest, and it settles in layers, as though slicing through rock, greeting each sedimentary level as it appears. At the top, where the canopy welcomes the blue and grey of the sky, it's awash with birdsong in the spring. So many voices, lifted higher as they serenade the dawn, greeting every new day as though it were the last one they'll ever live. Each evening, you could hear the almost reticent hush of bats' wings, as they fly in their circular hunting patterns, swooping and dancing in the dusk mists. Moving down from the canopy tops, the sounds become more muffled. Small creatures spend happy hours running from branch to branch, twig to twig, and the sounds of their footfalls are deadened by the gentle carpets of moss clinging to the boughs… like a covering of icing upon a spindly cake. In the autumn, when the leaves change from their vibrant greens to their oranges and yellows and reds, there's a kind of soft melody as each creature speaks to its companions. They chatter, or chirp, and they squeak, or they murmur. They're speaking of the passing season and they're speaking of how to gather food and keep themselves safe and warm as the time passes to colder weather. It's a beautiful resonance, in time and in tune with the woods. Always present, always dependable.

On the forest floor, there's so much to hear. So many sounds, and they all meld into one, if you don't know what to listen for. To the more astute ear, they are distinct and individual. Listen closely and you will pick out the voles, and the foxes; the badgers and, if you're very lucky, sometimes a lone pine marten. Such are the sounds of the woods. A beautiful symphony of languages, spoken in near silence, but audible to those who care to listen.

There's always been a certainty about the forest, but something was amiss that day.

Light changes as the seasons move. I saw the years pass; each one divided into its perfect pattern. I understood the movement of time, as my permanence allowed. It's been a privilege to stand firm here and watch life and death moving along in a never-ending cycle, and I remind myself how lucky I am to bear witness. I'm always enchanted by the light. You wouldn't think of light as such a spectrum, but it really is. The incredibly beautiful dappled light that peeks through the canopy atop is mesmerising. If you look upwards towards the skies, it sparkles and dances before you, illuminating the leaves and making them bright jewels, flashing their myriad of colours.

I'm forever aware of the dawn, as she creeps through the branches of the trees and the fullness of the bushes of the understorey. Ghost-like, she comes, opening her arms to the world as she greets all living things with her warmth, and a cloak of sunlight as she opens her arms and flings back the folds to reveal the light within. There is a solidity, a surety about her coming. Reassuring in her arrival, the forest life warms to her embrace and wakes anew, each day. That day was unusual, though, and everyone felt as though something was about to happen… almost as if dawn herself was hesitant to awaken the world.

I'm reminded of the time when I saw them, those two lovers… delicately caressing one another, whilst the gentle breeze coiled its way around their bodies, offering its gentle kiss upon their skin, each hair on end as they both shivered beneath its cool embrace. I could feel them on the moist ground, as they switched places, each one so desperate to fulfil that secret longing, and each one confident in the surety of their forbidden love. They didn't notice me. They didn't see me there, fastened to the earth, unable to move and unable to pull myself from the spot on which I stood. They didn't notice my gentle movement, almost in time with theirs…

Throughout time, I've seen so many lovers. They come and go, taking in the heady fragrance of the glade. There are bluebells, with their intoxicating scent. As they move though the flowers, taking care not to crush the stems, I'd see them pick one or two, and warmly brush the flower across their lover's cheek, whispering something and laughing. I'd see them lie down amongst the pale blueish purple carpet. Always in May, always in the spring. The bluebells never last too long, but they too saw those lovers, dancing their dance of desire. But only for a short while. Like love, momentary and fleeting, they draw deep on the potent thick air of the forest and become almost tipsy with it.

Honeysuckle winds its way through the shrubs and gives the air a sweetness, which is almost overpowering. Their pale cream trumpets are resplendent, and yet there is a coyness about the gently blushing flush to the petals... as though the entwined lovers have kissed just a little too passionately for the delicate flowers.

The brambles smell so sweet in the summertime. Large and swollen with life, they spill their deep purple ink onto unsuspecting fingers, as they pluck the fruits from the branches. I often watched as the mother and child wandered along the pathways, gently tugging the fruits, gleefully popping one into a container, one into their mouth, one in the pot, one in the mouth... The children had always run past me, and shouted out to each other, with happiness and excitement. I could see them playing their games and their pretences. Sometimes, they're spies or soldiers. Other times, they're princesses caught in a web of intrigue and waiting for some dragon to fly in and rescue them from the evil witch. The witch never wins. She's almost always ugly, with a cackle as vivid and as discordant as you can imagine. The children delight me, with their energy and their capacity for fun and love of life. Always rushing, always jumping and running, and laughing and singing. There's such innocence and joy, which I know will fade as they grow. It saddens me, as I see them each year…

I recognised them, and as each year passed, I witnessed the gentle erosion of joy upon their faces, as though a tiredness or ennui creeps upon them, like a wraith emerging from the shadows. The same faces for a while, and then nothing. Until new faces arrived in the woods, and the happy cycle started anew.

There were dogs too. They'd come and go, sniffing around. Sometimes they arrived at my feet with their noses pressed intently to the ground. Snuffling and overturning leaves and twigs, as if searching for that enigmatic lost bone from weeks before… never finding it, but the search is most of the fun. That search is all consuming, and should they ever find that special bone, then the search would be over and that always seems like such a disappointment. There were big dogs, on leads, with their masters or mistresses guiding them along a well-worn path. Trodden by hundreds of pairs of feet over time. They'd look up towards their walker, with love and devotion in their expressive faces. They're rewarded with a tickle or a scratch and a loving word or two. There were small ones too, often off leads, allowed to roam and bound and run freely through the undergrowth. Weaving from side to side along the path in front and to the side of me. I watched them, lifting their heads, sniffing the air. Unlike the lovers, they're not breathing in the intoxicating aroma of love making and desire, mixed with that scent of the bluebells… they're sniffing for that far away hint of a deep baked steak pie coming from the window of the old woman who lived on the outskirts. She baked daily, making her meal from home grown vegetables, and the beef she bought at the market in the town. She was never visited by her family, I noticed, and seemed to have a solitary existence, which she appeared to be happy with. I saw her walk along the same path, wearing her boots and her long coat, with pockets often stuffed with nuts and berries of the autumn. Beech nuts, hazelnuts, often rosehips and sweet chestnuts, and all sorts of berries are hanging from bushes and boughs, groaning under the weight of the autumnal bounty. So, the dogs sniffed the air, always, and I saw them try to make their way to the source of the feast, never really making it as their owners called to them to dissuade them from straying too far from the path.

Where were they that day? Noticeable in their absence, it made me feel as though things were changing. Right in front of us…

Often, I saw walkers, in pairs, generally. Old gentlemen with their flat caps and stout shoes. Chatting sternly to their comrade, as though solving all the world's riddles in that one moment in time, on that single morning walk. Finalising the details of later meetings. The time and the place, and not much more than that. There's a difference between the men and the women, in their chat. The women gossiped and laughed and shared secret jokes about their lovers, or their children, or the chap in the post office who always wears a blue tie with a pattern that looks like, well, you know…

Sometimes there was a covering of snow. Gently falling as it reached me, and made a sparkling carpet of brightness, which illuminated everything with an ethereal glow. When the sun splits through the canopy up above, shards of light bounce off the white vellum sheet, which delicately shrouds all that lays beneath. Light is not just white light, but a whole range of colour, and each leaf or petal, or shiny beetle back takes on a different hue, depending upon the time of day, or whether there is a slight cover of cloud above. I could often feel my skin absorb the light play, and it felt organic and freeing. The coolness and crispness of the air altered my appearance, and each tiny cell of my being reacted in a different way in the changing seasons. During the snowfall, I could feel my skin darken and harden somewhat, as it endeavoured to protect itself from the cold. I needed to feel this, as it reminded me of the years I've stood there and watched time pass… watched the children grow, watched the seasons move from one to the next, to the next…

In the woods, and everything was still and calm. Until the arrival of men with hats on, and yellow jackets. They stood and looked upwards, nodding to each other. I could see them talking and pointing and making notes on large wooden clipboards, with pens with chewed ends. More people arrived and disturbed my peace. I'd always felt grounded and, as the years rolled by, I'd never questioned the forest, never thought about its permanence. Not until that day.

These new beings had never appeared in the forest

before. Back when I was young, it seems like so long ago now, I only ever saw the lovers... so many lovers in this wood, over time. As the ages slipped by, their costumes changed, but not their desire. Desire is timeless, and love is ageless. They hugged me from time to time, wrapping their arms around me as if to never let go. Inhaling my scent, they laughed and cried and were joyful, but also sad and melancholic at times. But always they held me, or held each other.

These new people were strange to me. Back when I was young, hundreds of years, it seems, I only ever saw the children. They used fallen branches and boughs as weapons for horseplay... bows and arrows once, but now more as javelins or walking sticks to mimic their elders. Or to build little shelters in which to hide and eat their sandwiches and fallen fruit. They, too, hugged me from time to time. Joining their shorter arms together, they formed a ring around my middle and I felt their joy and their life as they connected with the earth.

But not today. Today is full of strangeness and uncertainty.

They brush past me, and I can feel their weight as they lean in. Seeing their breath in the coolness of the morning mists, I shudder slightly, and my bareness feels naked and vulnerable. At this time of year, I'm in a constant battle to keep my warmth inside, and it takes every ounce of effort to survive the wintertime, with its cold ravages. I don't like this. There's a strange atmosphere and I can feel my friends murmuring and shuddering around me. They're speaking to me in words that I understand... a language so ancient and unknown these days. We have spoken it to each other for so long that I cannot remember even learning it as a child. Our forebears teach us, and we learn and grow and ensure that our children, and theirs in turn, learn this unspoken speech.

Looking on either side of me, I see them, wandering and rubbing their chins. And then, through the break in the shrubs, on foot, I see more arrive, but they are calm and peaceful and have a sense of empathy about them. They speak in gentler tones, and they hold hands with each other. One is tall and willowy, with flame red hair, and he places his hand upon my side. I can feel the warmth bleed from his palm, and it seeps into me, like a warm rainfall on a summer's evening. It's refreshing and charging and gives me a feeling of ease. Another is smaller and stockier, with a child attached to her side. The child is smiling, and I see its mother stroking its face with a calmness and gentleness that throws me off guard. They, too, place their hands upon me, and the child's is small but warm, and I can feel an energy flow, a kind of vibration.

I've been here for so long now that I can remember every motion, every movement, every tiny vibration from all things. As time has passed, and I approach the twilight of my years, I'm trying to recall how many summers I've seen. Hundreds, I imagine. As time has passed, my life has been strong and powerful, and I have given life to many different animals and species. The light has entered my leaves and I have shivered and bent in the winds of autumn, they've felt heavy under layers of snow. They've fallen to the forest floor, sometimes gently, along with the sweet breezes of late summer. Sometimes violently, as the raging winds from the North have punched their path through the boughs with the force of a diving kestrel.

★

There's nothing left to be done now. I am old. I am older than that. I am ancient, it seems. Perhaps I would have lived for longer. But the air that I breathe is no longer ripe with life-giving power, no longer sustaining. There's a strange hum, now. Not the low hum of the forest, but a regular droning sound, palpable and discordant. I have no reference to where it is coming from, but I know from the others that it's not just me who hears it.

The men in yellow jackets are touching me. They speak softly to each other, with their heads almost touching. I can hear their sighs, and they sound saddened. The willowy man and his family stand close, and they press themselves up against my middle. I can feel their hands and their faces up against me, and it feels good. I know it is time. I realise there's no way out now. I am dying. I've stood here for such a long time, but I know there is no more time for me now.

I see the vehicles arrive. There are more people, and they alight, wearing boots and jackets and hats. They carry things in their hands, which look like paddles from the little dinghies that bob up and down on the water to the right of me. Families who have come and shared laughter and joy upon the little river that winds its way along the edge of the woods sometimes forget that we are here, I think. It's joyful to watch them delight in the beauty of this place…

The paddle type implements are for digging, it seems. There are a few people digging now. They're using so much energy and I can see them sweating as they plunge their devices into the ground. I'm uneasy.

But then, I see more of them arrive with large shiny black bulbs. Each carrying a large globe of glossy black material. What is happening in this place? For some reason, I feel at peace. As I watch them, carrying their globes, I can see each one has a twig, a branch, a bough… beautiful, something full of life…

★

The green shoots of new leaf growth peered through brown sheaths on the pale and dappled branches. There were rows and rows of them now. Each one arrived in a compostable bag. Each one lovingly planted by the guardians of the forest. So many of them turned up that day and cleared the forest floor where it meets the hedgerow. People with children arrived, holding shovels and they laughed and danced, and the children skipped along the pathways, as they held their faces up to the light.

★

"Mummy! Look!" the little boy called to his mother. She could see him pointing to the old tree.

"Isn't it beautiful, Jake? That's an old yew tree. Look

how magnificent it was." She gently touched the faded reddish-brown bark, which looked so old and had seen much life.

"So sad it's died, now, Mummy."

"Yes, but all things must die, so that new life can live."

As they walked through the woods and their feet trod the same well-worn paths, new life burst forth and the new, yearning and forceful branches leaned towards the sun at the canopy top, the dappled sunlight shining through, illuminating their leaves.

New life.

★★★

Samantha Latimer lives in Lancashire with her husband and kids and has a jewellery making business. She always wanted to be a writer, but life always seemed to get in the way, so taking part in this project has reignited that spark.

You can find out more about her jewellery here:
https://www.instagram.com/samanthalatimerjewellery/
https://www.facebook.com/samanthalatimerjewellery

THE WINDFALL

Hayley Dartnell

The clock on the wall in the black and white tiled hallway of the Victorian house ticked gently. It was ten past eight on a cold, wet and miserable Monday morning.

"Hurry up, you two, we'll be late for school!" Sophie yelled up the stairs to her children, Michael aged thirteen and her daughter Darcey, who had just turned nine.

Glancing through a clear square of the stained-glass window, she spotted the postman out on his deliveries coming up the garden path. Pulling on her old béige raincoat, a large handful of post was pushed through the letterbox. The mixture of envelopes and leaflets landed on the mat with a shuffle. Scooping up the pile, Sophie eyeballed the stack of final demands, opened the lid of the grey upholstered ottoman and shoved them in. A job for later, she thought, as her heart raced in anticipation, dropping the takeaway and double-glazing flyers into the tall metal bin, once used for umbrellas. She eagerly tore open a smart white envelope of news she had been waiting for, but her hope of receiving a job acceptance was dashed once more. She had lost track of exactly how many interviews she'd attended in the past few months and the rejection letters almost outweighed the number of final demands that arrived on a daily basis. Sophie's eyes filled with tears, and she wiped them briskly away with the back of her sleeve as she read the disappointing outcome of last Wednesday's informal chat with a local accountancy firm looking to recruit an administrator. Another complete waste of time, she thought, balling up the useless piece of paper and hurling it at the front door in frustration. Reaching over to the coat peg on the wall behind her, she yanked off a pretty cotton scarf and wound it furiously around her neck, trapping her long chestnut-coloured hair in the process. Catching her sad reflection in the mirror, her face was devoid of makeup and dark circles under her tired bloodshot eyes only highlighted her despair. Sophie felt absolutely wretched. How on earth were they going to manage?

It had been just over a year since her husband Alex of fifteen years had walked out and left them all penniless. He'd taken off two days after Christmas with a female colleague from his office, leaving Sophie with a mountain of debt to pay. The credit card repayments alone were crippling but the mortgage on their beautifully renovated Victorian semi in the nicer part of Clapham was just as expensive. Sophie had never been in charge of the household finances, Alex had always taken care of their money, being the sole 'breadwinner'. It had made Sophie feel safe and content to be a stay at home mum. But since

Alex's departure, bills started arriving. The email address Alex had provided no longer existed, therefore each creditor had written to Sophie instead to find another way of retrieving their money. Sophie had endured the painful task of going through the huge stack of unopened mail one Saturday evening whilst the kids were at a sleepover. She had made a list of everyone they owed money to and, when dawn broke, found herself waking up at the kitchen table, surrounded by paperwork with a biro in her hand.

Sophie had told no one how dire the situation had become, not even her parents, both retired artists who resided in a very small remote hamlet in a rural part of Cornwall. Finally realising that she needed to share the burden with someone, Sophie reached for the phone. With a heavy heart, she placed a call to her best friend Pat. It would be a call that would change her life forever.

Pat, a former escort with a voice that could mimic any accent in the world, had been servicing the rich and famous in more ways than one for the past twenty years. She had taken early retirement from the escort business just before her forty-second birthday, after a regular client had suggested she invest in a boob job. Pat had gazed forlornly at her once magnificent bosom and considered her client's generous offer to pay for the surgery at a private London clinic. The once tight youthful skin bore an abundance of visible stretch marks that extended up to her neckline, due to excessive sunbathing on foreign holidays. Her breasts were now suddenly making their own way south on the quickest route to Brighton. So, with that incentive, she shut up shop and opened a new one with the help of her friend Joe, in one of London's most desirable streets, near St James's. A very exclusive ladies' designer boutique, aimed at the elite and those with more money to spend than actual common sense. Pat had even gone as far as to pop a small brass sign in the window saying 'By Appointment Only' just to add to the whole pompousness of it all, and sure enough, it had worked. Word had spread and the telephone had not stopped ringing with customers eager to step inside the luxurious converted townhouse.

The spacious ground floor was filled with expensive gowns, couture dresses, designer handbags, tiny diamond trinkets and a stunning dressing area. The upper floors were her living quarters and occasionally she rented out the tiny self-contained studio flat in the basement during the summer months for extra income. When Sophie had telephoned that Sunday morning and explained her predicament, Pat had been doing inventory in the boutique. She immediately dropped everything, jumped into a black cab and made a pitstop at the local deli.

Over takeaway lattes, Sophie explained the true extent of her financial problems. Pat wished she had brought wine instead, they clearly needed something far stronger than coffee. Copious amounts of alcohol would not solve this problem, though, but neither would Sophie entering into the escort world, which is what she was hoping to do. Pat was horrified. She tried everything in her power to dissuade Sophie from venturing down the sex trade path, pointing out all the pitfalls and the overall danger. Sophie had kids, this was a ludicrous idea.

"Just let me write you a cheque, I'll pay off the credit cards at least," Pat had pleaded. But Sophie was adamant. She needed the money and would stop at nothing to provide for her family.

After several heated arguments, Pat very reluctantly put Sophie in touch with a former colleague who promised to ease her gently into 'the business'. It meant going out with men and women for social lunches, dinner or drinks, simply as a companion to begin with. As Sophie's confidence grew, she began getting regular bookings, all sexually related, with the potential to earn more money in a few hours than some people could working a whole week stacking shelves in a supermarket. With Pat's help, Sophie borrowed makeup, designer clothes and accessories from the boutique on the days she had a client. But Pat knew this lifestyle was not suited to Sophie. She didn't have the temperament or the street smarts for it. Pat was all too aware of how a straightforward client could easily turn into a psychopath at the flick of a switch. On more than one occasion she had been in that position herself. Pat wasn't prepared to let that happen, so she came up with a suitable plan to free Sophie from the escort world and put an end to her money worries once and for all. She just needed help from one person. Joe.

Pat's friendship with Joe began just over ten years ago in Notting Hill. They had met at a party, hosted by a television celebrity. Pat was working and her date for the evening was a promising young musical theatre actor whilst Joe was delivering narcotics to the host. He was part of London's underworld, most of it involving drugs, alcohol and stolen goods. The only legitimate business he had was an expensive deli just off Haymarket, which provided the perfect decoy for the seedy operation that he ran.

When Pat mentioned the idea of leaving the escort business behind and opening up an exclusive boutique, Joe was delighted and purchased the town house for her. Pat knew all about his dodgy dealings and where the money had come from to fund her new venture, but she wasn't put off in the slightest. They were like two peas in a pod most of the time and she loved to keep him on his toes. Especially one day back in the summer, when she managed to almost knock him off his feet quite literally.

"You want me to do what?" Joe asked, his voice almost a whisper.

"I need you to kill Alex please," Pat repeated calmly and slowly, just in case he hadn't heard her properly the first time.

Never in his wildest dreams did he ever think she of all people would ask this type of favour from him. He marched heavy footed through to the back of the boutique and sank heavily onto a chair in the tiny galley kitchen. Nothing usually fazed him being in his line of work. But murder?

"I assume you have a plan?" Joe continued patiently. Pat sat down on the chair opposite and nodded excitedly.

As summer crept into autumn, Sophie had accrued a few regulars, but her income was barely keeping the wolf from her front door. This morning she was back in the beautiful hotel near Piccadilly Circus. Same man, same time and even the same king-sized bed, lying comfortably on freshly pressed Egyptian cotton sheets with her overweight sweaty regular thrusting happily away. Not that she could really feel him inside her, he was hung like a cold mouse on a wet day. This was one of Pat's favourite expressions used to describe a past client and it always made Sophie giggle. Today was no exception and she had to gulp back the snigger, so her client didn't notice. He was beginning to grunt now, a sure sign he was about to ejaculate. It's about time, thought Sophie with relief, thinking she might have to thrust a finger up his arse to get things moving a bit quicker, a superb trick she had learnt recently.

Sophie glanced discreetly at her watch. She needed to call into Pat's boutique on her way to her next client in Knightsbridge to return a beautiful full-length black cashmere coat that she had borrowed last week. The Uber she had booked was due in fifteen minutes, so there was just enough time to drop off the garment before her next appointment across town.

With one final thrust, the man screwed up his face and pulled out his tiny manhood. He quickly removed the coloured condom he was wearing and ejaculated onto Sophie's bare stomach. They both watched as a tiny trickle of semen leaked slowly from his shrivelling penis and dripped into her belly button. Reaching across to the nightstand, he plucked out a handful of tissues from a mirrored box, passing them to Sophie before heading to the bathroom.

Wiping away the sticky fluid, she deposited the tissues

into the small waste bin by the antique desk and delved into her large designer tote, a birthday gift from Pat, for a packet of baby wipes. She cleaned herself up, dumping the used cloths into the same bin, and spritzed herself with a copy of a well-known floral perfume she'd found on a market stall for a few quid. Dragging a brush through her hair, she secured it with a clip and retrieved her tailored black trouser suit and nude-coloured blouse from a chair, dressing quickly. Picking up her tote and the garment bag, she pocketed her fee, an envelope stuffed with cash left on a small antique sideboard. She called out a polite goodbye to indicate she was leaving and closed the heavy mahogany door quietly behind her. There was no small talk with this client. Just a once-a-week session of on your back, no frills sex, thank goodness. But she was grateful for the money, as it was keeping a roof over their heads and food on the table, no matter how much it made her skin crawl. She was doing it for her children. Darcey needed new school shoes and the plan was to buy some at half term if she could scrape enough money together. But another worry had reared its ugly head. The previous week, over a budget meal of fish fingers, homemade chips and spaghetti hoops, Michael had asked a question she had been dreading.

"Is Dad ever coming home?" he asked, in a very quiet voice as he speared a chip from his plate, sitting at his favoured end of the kitchen table.

Sophie couldn't lie, and explained in the kindest way possible that she simply didn't know. Michael had shrugged his shoulders and thanked her for being honest. Sophie almost burst into tears on the spot as her brave young son tried to act all grown up in front of her. Michael clearly missed his father, whereas Darcey not as much. She was a mummy's girl but adored her big brother. She put down a droopy fish finger that was dangling off her fork, dripping with watery ketchup, and went to put her arms around Michael's neck.

"It's okay, you have us," said Darcey with a grin, squeezing him tightly. "Doesn't he, Mum?" Sophie pushed away her own plate of food and went to hug her children.

Sophie was thinking of Michael's question again when she arrived home. She ran up the stairs to her en suite, tossing her clothes into the laundry basket, making a beeline for a much-needed shower before the school run. The hot soapy water pulsated over her slender body, cleansing her stretch marks from having two beautiful children and washing away the grubbiness from her client, a wealthy banker. Sophie shuddered, remembering his gentle hands delicately caressing the inside of her milky thighs, then thought of the generous tip he had pushed into her small hand. She was grateful of the extra fifty-pound note, it would cover the minimum payments on the credit cards that were due and stretch to a tub of ice cream as a treat. There hadn't been many of those lately. She sighed, pulling on a comfy pair of jeans and an old grey jumper. With her money worries weighing constantly on her mind, there was the real possibility they would lose the house in the next few months. Another letter from the bank had arrived in the second post and confirmed her suspicions.

Approaching the school gates, a text message from Pat lit up her screen. A smiley face, a glass of red wine and a thumbs up emoji confirmed their plans for later. There hadn't been time to chat when she called in at the boutique to drop off the coat, but Pat had seen the anxious look in Sophie's eyes and suggested coming over after dinner.

Final demands for all the outstanding bills were coming in faster than ever. When the creditors had begun asking her to increase her monthly payments, a few had turned quite nasty. She retaliated to their threats by threatening to declare bankruptcy. They retreated for a few weeks but they weren't giving up. They just wanted their money back. The bank had already said her overdraft facility would not be extended and, with Christmas just around the corner, this was the last thing Sophie needed.

Plucking two dusty wine glasses from a cupboard, she gave them a wipe with a clean dry cloth just as Pat's theatrical voice floated down the stairs, followed by a round of applause and cheering. Pat had finished the last chapter of *The Escape*, a brand new children's fairy tale from the series called *The Lavender Fairy Adventures*, a book that Darcey had desperately wanted because all her friends had a copy. It was the latest trend at school, having just hit all the major bookshops in the United Kingdom. But Sophie simply couldn't afford to buy it. To avoid another argument with her daughter, she had mentioned it to Pat, who very kindly stepped in and purchased a special edition from a well-known bookshop on Charing Cross Road. Michael had protested that he was far too old for a story but he could never resist a tale read by Auntie Pat. With both children finally tucked up in bed, Sophie poured two generous glasses of Merlot from the bottle Pat had brought.

"Cheers!" they both said in unison, chinking their glasses, but a moment later Sophie was in floods of tears. By way of explanation, she showed Pat the latest letter from the bank about the house.

Seeing her friend in this much distress was heartbreaking. Pat just hoped that the plan she had put in place was going to work.

"Come on, girl, just hang in there," Pat had whispered gently. "You never know what's around the corner."

A week later, it was Halloween. Darcey stood dressed up in the hallway waiting to go out 'Trick or Treating' with her best friend, looking like a carbon copy of Hermione, her favourite character from the Harry Potter movies. Michael didn't want to go out and was happily ensconced up in his bedroom with his best friend Blake, a bowl of popcorn and a games console.

Sophie watched her youngest walk down the path, arm in arm with Tilly, from the living room window, then she settled herself on the overstuffed sofa and tuned into the teatime news.

The headline was of a multi-vehicle car crash on the M25 near Lakeside, involving a lorry and causing a twelve-mile hold up of traffic. A chill ran down Sophie's back as the newsreader announced there had only been one fatality, just as the cameraman zoomed in on a close up shot of a crumpled Chelsea Tractor. A shiny black four by four that had been stolen earlier that day from an area in East London, with a child's seat in the back. She shuddered at the thought of losing one of her children, or worse still both of them to a car accident, but the sombre journalist was quick to point out there was no one else in the car apart from the driver. CCTV footage had revealed the luxury BMW was racing against an unmarked sports car who had swerved to avoid the crash. It went on to say that Kent Police were conducting a full investigation into the accident and were keen to track down the other driver. Alex had always driven like a maniac and never liked to be overtaken, especially on the motorway or by a woman. He couldn't sit in traffic either, his hand would be permanently on the horn yelling extremities out of the window.

The doorbell shrilled loudly, making her jump, swiftly cutting off her train of thought and signalling the first of many 'Trick or Treaters' that would be doing the rounds of the neighbourhood. Flicking off the TV, she picked the pumpkin-style bucket filled with sweets that Pat had thoughtfully dropped off the week before and opened the front door with a smile.

The very next day, Steve, Pat's regular postman, called in at the boutique. "Morning love!" he bellowed cheerfully as she opened the front door. He vigorously wiped his heavy boots on the large in-built mat before walking across the polished wooden floor and through to the back. Picking up the daily newspaper folded in half on the kitchen table, the ugly headline splashed across it read: 'Halloween Nightmare on M25.'

"Unbelievable, isn't it? Only one fatality in that massive pile up last night!" Steve exclaimed, shaking his head. Putting the newspaper back where he found it, he handed Pat a bundle of letters and a clipboard. "Says here they're calling it an accident. Some bloke, apparently, let's hope he didn't have any kids, eh?" he continued in his cockney twang.

"Unbelievable," Pat repeated, trying her utmost not to beam with happiness as she signed her name in the allocated box with a flourish. Eager to finish his rounds, Steve bid Pat his usual farewell and held open the front door, allowing Joe to step over the threshold of the boutique carrying a crate of champagne.

Placing the bottles on top of the newspaper, he turned to face Pat. She was beaming with happiness and threw her arms around his neck, shrieking the words, "Thank you, thank you!" into his right ear. Puzzled at this sudden outburst of affection, he returned her hug. "What for, love?" he enquired.

Wriggling from his embrace, Pat yanked out the newspaper from under the crate and pointed at the headline. Joe had to come clean. "I couldn't do it," he confessed quietly, unable to look her in the eye.

Sophie had just returned home from the school run when there was a knock at the door. Two uniformed police officers greeted her with sombre smiles. Immediately jumping to conclusions, Sophie thought she was being arrested for not paying the council tax bill and promptly burst into tears until the female officer interjected with a soothing voice.

"Mrs Briars, we're here on a rather sensitive matter." Her features softened at Sophie's distress. "Please, may we come in?"

The news of Alex's death was still sinking in as Sophie tipped three mugs of cold tea down the sink. Alex had been formally identified by his parents as the driver of the black four by four that had crashed on the M25, killing him instantly. The first call she made was to the school informing them she was on her way to pick up the children. She then tried Pat and her parents, but both calls went straight to voicemail. Hanging up the phone, she stared out of the bi-folds into the garden. The ridiculously expensive doors that Alex had insisted they had needed to complete their extension. Frowning at the memory, she bolted for the downstairs loo as a thick bile rose up suddenly from the bottom of her stomach.

Telling the children was another matter. Darcey had immediately started crying, whereas Michael frowned and sat perfectly still on the sofa in the kitchen, with his arms tightly crossed. Sophie reached out to cuddle him, but he just shrugged her off and ran upstairs to his room, slamming the door behind him.

Six weeks later, Sophie had just finished decorating the tall and bushy artificial Christmas tree in the living room, hoping the pretty white lights might cheer them all up. Sadly not. Michael was still very angry at the loss of his father but he'd also seen a letter from the bank that Sophie had forgotten to hide. Their house was being repossessed in the new year if the balance wasn't paid in full by the end of December.

Waking up from a broken night's sleep on Christmas Eve morning, Sophie heard the letterbox clatter. The kids were still fast asleep and seeing as there was no reason to wake them just yet, she pulled on her towelling dressing gown and padded downstairs, stopping to pick up the only piece of mail on her way to the kitchen. A hand delivered envelope with her name on it.

Assuming it was just a Christmas card from a neighbour, she carefully opened it, pausing to admire the hand-illustrated snowy scene of a very small mouse perched on a thin blade of grass in a pretty woodland setting. She was wondering who it was from when two items fell to the floor. A business card that she instantly recognised from the hotel near Piccadilly Circus, the other a neatly folded cheque for one million pounds. The message inside the card simply read: 'Merry Christmas Sophie'.

★★★

Hayley lives in Cambridgeshire. Her passion for writing is based upon nature, true events and real locations. All her stories have fairy tale endings as well.

You can purchase her children's book *The Escape* (the first in the 'Lavender Fairy Adventures' series) here: https://www.amazon.co.uk/Escape-Lavender-Fairy-Adventures/dp/1916114792

WISH UPON
A FALLING STAR

Richard Dee

"It's always the dog walkers," said Jarman.

Detective Inspector Parkhill agreed, although it wouldn't do to encourage his junior too much. He stopped the car at the yellow tape barrier that had been set up at the edge of the car park. Around him, a couple of journalists and some early morning customers, denied their breakfast at the beach café, jostled for a view. They were so engrossed in what was happening that they had failed to notice his arrival. The subject of their interest was thirty yards away, out of sight behind the ambulance and down the steps to the beach.

Parkhill sighed, another day, another body. Summer was like that on the south coast. People came to the sea late at night, swimming after too much alcohol. It meant that, at the best time of the year, he was working too hard picking up the pieces to enjoy the good weather. Why did they leave their common sense at home when they came on holiday? It was sad but true; Jarman was right. Dog walkers found the majority of the victims, they even saved some of them.

"What would we do without them?" Parker said as he turned the engine off. At least they had called an ambulance and not the newspapers. The two policemen pushed through the scrum, making no comment to all the shouted questions. This was the first body of the week. The last two days had been taken up with the aftermath of the shooting star. That had been mostly seen by dog walkers too, flashing across the early morning sky and apparently landing in the sea. If it had hit the land, there would have been a lot more paperwork. As it was, there was nothing to see; any bits of the meteor were safely underwater and there hadn't been a tsunami. Small mercies, normal service could be resumed.

The local press had made a big thing of it, the nationals had got involved, there had been sightings in a line across the country, even some shaky mobile phone footage. But now it was old news, replaced by the next big thing. Jarman headed to the beach while Parkhill was led to a pair of elderly people standing nervously with a large white retriever. "This is Mr and Mrs Lerner," the constable said.

"Good morning," said Parkhill, "thank you for staying here."

"That's fine," said the man, "we wanted to make sure that he got help."

"Well, it's appreciated. I will need a proper statement from you. But, if you can briefly tell me what happened, that'll do for the moment."

"Sir," called Jarman, "you're needed on the beach."

Parkhill cursed; couldn't Jarman do anything without checking?

"I'm sorry," he said. "Please be patient and I'll come back to you just as soon as I've seen what's going on." He walked down the steps and followed Jarman along the beach to the body, which was lying between some rocks.

"He's still alive, unconscious but the paramedics say he's not seriously hurt," Jarman said.

The paramedics had stabilised him, a neck collar was fitted, the stretcher ready to lift him to the waiting ambulance. Around the scene, uniformed men peered into the gaps between the rocks. The café owner shuffled about, wanting to speak but trying to avoid sounding indifferent. "He wants to know when he can open up," said Jarman. "I told him to be patient."

Parkhill nodded his understanding, business was business. "Any identification?"

Jarman shook his head. "Not here, although we're still looking." Usually, they left a pile of clothes with all their gear before they went for the midnight swim that took their lives.

"Nothing so far, sir," said one of the uniforms. "We've checked all around the rocks."

"Try the next bay on either side," said Parkhill. "He might have been swept around."

Parkhill turned back to the body. Young and slim with good muscle definition. Close cropped blond hair. Fine down covering his back. Lots of bruising, a few scratches but no deep cuts. "Not even a broken bone, no dislocations," said one of the paramedics. That was strange, he had been deposited on the shore by the waves, yet he was not badly hurt. It meant he had been lucky. The eyes were closed. He looked peaceful, asleep, the chest rising and falling gently. "Can we take him?" asked the paramedic.

"I've got lots of pictures," said the police photographer. "Closeups of the face – I thought you might need them for canvassing."

"Okay," said Parkhill to the paramedics, "he's all yours. We can come along and question him when he wakes up."

He went back to the couple. "Sorry about that. Now, in your own words, please tell me what happened this morning."

★

The story was long and convoluted, told with many asides and finishing of each other's sentences. Parkhill didn't mind. He had found it best to let people talk, interruptions confused them, led them off on a tangent. They would have to complete written statements later. He let them tell the story in their own way, filing away the important points. Jarman would probably have rushed them, interrupted them, got them confused.

He learned that Tim and Sylvia Lerner always walked Skipper, the Labrador, in the morning, just after the beach café opened. Then they had coffee and chatted to the other dog walkers before the crowds arrived on the beach. It was only ten minutes' walk from their bungalow, a bit of a trek back up the hill afterwards but worth it for the views, and the exercise a good excuse for a cake to go with their coffee.

This morning, the talk among the walkers who they saw every day was of the shooting star, two days ago. Someone they called Maud had been taking her spaniel for an early stroll and had seen it pass almost directly overhead, before plunging into the sea, about three miles offshore, she reckoned. Yesterday, she had explained it all to anyone who would listen, waving her arms to indicate the motion. 'I was in the *Herald*', she had told them, 'they reckoned that the T.V. people might turn up to interview me but nothing happened'.

"We were earlier today," said Tim, getting back to the matter in hand. "The café was still closed. Skipper's getting old and rarely runs, although he loves a swim. As we passed the café; we came to the rocks that fell last winter. They block the best part of the beach."

"We were about to turn back," said Sylvia, taking over the story, "then, Skipper suddenly set off, barking loudly."

"He must have spotted something," said Tim. "We were hoping that it wasn't another dead fish."

"I'm telling this bit," she scolded him. "He once found a part decomposed mackerel on the beach, he would not drop it, it made him stink for weeks afterwards, no matter what we did. We followed him and saw him standing over a dark shape, in among the rocks, just above the high tide line. As we got closer, we could see that it was a man."

"And what did you do then?" asked Parkhill.

"I felt for a pulse," she said. "Checked his airway. I was careful not to move him. Then I sent Tim to see if the café was open, call an ambulance and the police."

"And that was it?"

"Yes," she said. "It was hardly any time before the ambulance turned up, followed by the first of the policemen. Then you arrived."

"Thank you," he said, "you've done very well, probably saved his life. All we need now is your name and address; we'll be in touch for a proper statement."

They looked pleased, nodding. "It's only what anyone would do, we were just the first," Tim said.

"What will you do to identify him, if he doesn't wake up?" asked Sylvia.

"We'll put out pictures, try the local holiday camps and hotels. See if anyone's been reported missing."

"He's very distinctive, isn't he?" said Silvia. "Handsome. Someone is bound to know him."

I hope so, thought Parkhill, *a simple job would be nice.* Behind him, the stretcher containing the man was lifted into the ambulance.

★

The local hospital's Accident and Emergency department was used to receiving bodies pulled from the sea – fishermen, over-enthusiastic holidaymakers and drunk students convinced they were Olympic swimmers were run of the mill – so when the blond man arrived, it raised barely a ripple. Anyway, this one was breathing, had no obvious broken bones or internal trauma, so wasn't a priority. He was unconscious, which scored him a few points, and unidentified, which got him a few more. As he moved through the system, he was subjected to a barrage of tests and scans.

★

Later that day, Parkhill's phone rang. It was a welcome diversion from his paperwork. Jarman was busy checking for missing persons, armed with a photo of the mystery man.

"Parkhill," he answered.

"Hi," said a voice he recognised. Trish Upton worked in the hospital, a sister on one of the medical wards. He knew her well, they had shared enough night shifts, him trying to question suspects and victims, her trying to heal them. Once, there had been a spark between them, not so much now, the hours they worked had conspired to keep them apart. They were still good friends, though. Parkhill wondered why she was calling.

"Did you see the shooting star?" she asked, after the usual pleasantries.

"No," said Parkhill. "I was asleep. I've seen the film, though, it looked impressive."

"The papers said it was unusual to get that close. They normally burn up well before they reach the ground."

"It would have made a mess of Torbay," he said. "At least it landed in the sea."

Trish laughed. "We could have been busy if it hadn't."

There was a pause. "Trevor," she said, "were you involved with the man they found on the beach?"

"Yes, I was," he said, wondering why she would ask. "Have A & E finished with him?"

"They're sending him up to my tender care," she laughed. "There was a bit of a fuss down there."

"Really, he must have woken up then?"

"He did, that was when the fun started. He couldn't remember his name, or anything. Carol, one of the nurses, told me he got agitated. Apparently, there was a struggle. It got quite physical. Security guards were called, we had to restrain him. We haven't had one like that for ages."

Parkhill had seen the drunks and addicts, resisting treatment, hurting themselves and the people that were trying to help. He knew the government had legislated to allow physical restraints, in certain circumstances. He had to admit, it had saved nurses from injury, even though he thought it was a step too far. "Is he calm now?"

"I guess, we'll see when he gets here. I'm getting a single room ready for him, just in case."

"I'm coming in, Trish, I need to question him anyway; if he's awake, I might as well do it now. It might jog his memory."

"Be nice to see you," she said warmly. "I'll get the kettle on." Parkhill knew she wouldn't have time for that, but still, it would be good to see her again, it'd been a while. On his way out, he checked with Jarman. So far, nobody had been reported missing and nothing had been found at the scene.

★

"Hi Trish," said Parkhill, when he got her attention; the ward was busy, all the staff occupied. "Where's our mystery man?"

"He's in four," she said. "Still a bit groggy but we've had all the results now. Everything checks out. No broken bones, no internal injuries. He's been lucky, as far as we can tell it's just cuts and bruises."

"Does he remember anything?" Parkhill was still hoping for an easy job.

"We haven't asked again, that was where all the trouble started last time. New policy guidelines are not to provoke a response. We've hooked him up and left him alone. I've got more to worry about than questioning him. The psychs are on the way to assess him when they get a minute. Meanwhile, my instructions are that he stays secure."

"Why would he get so worked up, could it be concussion?"

"Maybe," she said, nodding. "It might have been panic when he found he couldn't remember anything. His brain function seems okay, no bleeds are showing on the scan, it'll all come back to him in the end."

"We can't help him," Parkhill said, "at least not yet. There were no clues at the scene, no wallet, not even any clothes. Dog walkers found him."

"Good old dog walkers," she said. "A real mystery man. Very distinctive, though, quite handsome."

Parkhill smiled. She had called him that, once. "Let's go and say hello," he suggested.

*

When they entered the room, Parkhill could see that the man was calm. Good, he thought, that would make his job a lot easier. The mystery man was lying on his back, blue eyes gazing at the ceiling. Straps still held his hands and feet. One crossed his stomach. A monitor screen traced his vital signs, and there was a drip fitted in his left arm.

"What's in the drip?" asked Parkhill. He didn't want to mention the straps in front of the patient. "It's just saline, he's slightly dehydrated," explained Trish. "We don't know how long it's been since he ate or drank last. It could be affecting his memory."

"Hello, sir," Parkhill said softly. "I'm Detective Parkhill, can you hear me?"

"Yes," replied the man. "Where am I?" His voice was soft; hesitant, as if he was searching for the right words. He didn't sound aggressive, maybe he had calmed down.

"You're in Torbay hospital," Trish replied. "We found you on the shore at Oddicombe beach."

"I don't know where that is," said the man.

"Do you know your name, your address?" asked Parkhill. "Is there anyone who we can contact, a wife, parent? Please don't be alarmed, you're not in any trouble, we just want to know who you are, get you fit and home safe."

The man shook his head. "My name is… John." He said it with difficulty, as if dredging it up from the depths of his mind. "The rest, I don't know." His tone suggested desperation, the sudden realisation that he could remember nothing. He rattled the straps. "What's happened to me, why am I held down?"

"I'm sorry about that," she said. "Hospital policy. You got quite agitated when you first arrived. You needed examining. We had to put them on you to do it safely."

The man looked shocked. "I see," he said.

"What's the last thing you remember, John?" asked Parkhill.

"Falling," he replied, almost instantly. "Then water all around me." He struggled to rise, pulling against the straps. He was shouting now, "I have to get back, tell them what's happened, they'll be waiting, they need to know."

"Who? Tell me and I can tell them."

He fell back. "I can't…"

Trish stopped Parkhill at that point. "That's enough, Trevor. You rest, John, and don't worry, your memory will come back, just give it time."

Trish and Parkhill left the room. "It's a start," she said as the door closed on John. "We'll call you if anything changes. He'll be kept here until there's an assessment by the psychs. Then we can decide what to do with him."

"Thanks, Trish, I'll go and track my D.C. down, he's been taking a picture round. See you later." As he walked away, he considered all the possible ways of finding out this man's identity. So much for an easy job.

★

As the door closed, Jahan relaxed. His fear and sense of helplessness was replaced by calm and confidence. He was safe, at least for the immediate future. The bipeds hadn't seen through his disguise, the manufactured shell that concealed his true nature. None of the primitive medical equipment had detected that he was really Jahan from Theth.

Memory chips in his shell were filled with information on this world. The nanites had done a sterling job of repairs, since his involuntary soaking. All his systems were nearly back to full operation. He knew he could snap his bonds easily, the enhanced muscles he possessed were more than capable. But he had decided that it would not help him to do so.

He had bigger problems; his ship was gone, lost in the liquid water that abounded on this world. He had no way of telling his people that he lived, he would have to wait for another to come, hope for rescue. He knew that his mate on Theth and his cubs would grieve for him, he felt sorrow for their suffering.

If he had to stay in this place, he would have to adapt, quickly. He needed to find a biped to assist him. They could never know his true purpose, as the advance guard of a conquering race.

There was still plenty of information about the planet and its defences that the High Council needed, information that he could gather and store, ready to present when the time came. If he searched hard enough, he might even be able to fashion a means of communication, to let them know he was alive and still working for the cause. He thought of the bipeds he had seen so far, evaluated their usefulness, suitability.

There was Trish, the old female in the uniform. He dismissed her. He could see that she was suffering from a tumour. She would expire soon. He might have many of their years to wait. The detective then? No, he might grow suspicious of his actions.

The door opened again, he noticed a new scent in the room, some sort of flower overlaid the pheromones of a female.

"Hello, John," she called; it was the sound of a young voice. He noticed with interest that some of his shell's functions had changed at the sound. The pressure of the blood flow had increased, he felt his outer skin warming. The eyes seemed to take in more light, lung capacity increased by a little over... eight per cent.

"How are you feeling now?" she continued, making a clanking noise as she moved some hidden equipment. Jahan turned his head. She had her back to him, bending over to reach something. The part of his chips memory that had been constructed from human experiences told him that the bipeds regarded this view as pleasant.

"The doctor says that you're not from around here," she continued. "How do you like Devon?"

What was this effect, why did she make his body behave in this way? It was merely a construction of DNA and manufactured flesh, grown in a laboratory. All the human functions and memories were controlled by a processor chip in the shell. It was only supposed to cover his frame and change its appearance, making him acceptable to the bipeds. There was no intention to make it independently sentient, yet by some means, its nucleic acid was doing just that. He sensed an attraction for her; how had this body taken on emotion? It seemed to register parts of the consciousness of the humans, the ones who had been harvested to make it.

"It's very nice," he said. "I've never been in a place like this before." That, at least, was true.

"You should stay," she suggested. "I can help you find somewhere; until you get your memory back."

As if I have a choice, he thought.

She stood up, turned and Jahan saw her face for the first time. It was a different face to everyone else's, oval, tanned, surrounded by short hair and huge brown eyes. And her shell, it was more curved than his, more than the older females had been. It too was pleasant. He noted that her face was flushed. Her body seemed to be exhibiting the same changes as his. She must also be feeling the attraction. He felt his mouth move into a smile.

"Did you see the shooting star?" she asked. "Two nights ago, it was amazing."

"No," replied Jahan, "I don't think I did." He was unwilling to tell her that it wasn't a star, it was his ship, out of control and crashing into the sea.

"Oh well, never mind, there'll be others. My grandmother tells me, if you see one you should make a wish."

Jahan accessed the relevant memory, understanding the concept instantly. The nanites must have completed their repairs, his recall was now fully restored. Almost without realising it, he wished for his people to come and save him, take him back to his mate. Even while he thought it, he knew that wishful thinking would get him nowhere. He had to come up with another plan. Perhaps he could use the mutual attraction to his advantage. In return, as he was here, he could try to make her existence happy.

Then he wondered, why was he behaving like this? His shell was clearly affected by the female's presence, could it be influencing him? Should he feel such guilt, thinking of this biped in that way? Was he not Jahan, here as a conqueror, to take everything that he could from these primitives? Yet he was suddenly full of doubt. It was almost disloyal; he was happily mated, with cubs of his own. But that was on Theth, light-years distant. Was it just self-preservation that made him realise he was here, he had to blend in? Who knew when he would sit under the blood-red sun of Theth again?

She must have taken his silence for doubt. "Would you like me to help you, mysterious John?" she said. "Just until your memory returns; or your family arrive."

Jahan was aware that she was about the same age as he was designed to appear. She had many years ahead of her. All her systems were functioning properly. They could grow old together. Perhaps, a wait on this planet, in this Devon, might not be such a bad thing after all.

"I think that would be good," he replied.

★★★

Richard Dee is a retired Master Mariner and ship's pilot, living in Brixham, South Devon. Years spent travelling the real world inspired him to create new places and times for his characters to explore. His novels include Science Fiction and Steampunk adventures, as well as the exploits of Andorra Pett, a reluctant amateur detective. You can find out about his life and writing at https://richarddeescifi.co.uk/

THE MAN UPSTAIRS

Becky Leeson

Far too many people go missing these days. Some vanish into thin air, as if stepping into a magician's black cabinet. The act goes horribly wrong, and they never reappear. There's no big reveal, no red-faced bow to the crowd. Nothing.

Others choose to leave. They wake up one day and say, 'Do you know what? This isn't for me.' And that's it. There's no magic, no trickery involved. They slurp down their cup of tea, cram a few essentials into an overnight bag, and whistle on their way out. They're usually halfway across the country before realising they've forgotten to pack a toothbrush.

The girl on the front of the newspaper has been missing for some time now, all fat black print and a photo from happier times. She's pretty, too. They always use a nice photo when someone goes missing. To give a sense of who they were, before a traumatic event. Before the magician came along.

I say, show someone looking a little rough. Hungover, even. You just might find them burying their heads in the supermarket on a Sunday afternoon, shuffling past the chicken kievs and the fish fingers in a grey hoodie with two pints of milk and last night's headache.

Returning the newspaper to its rack, I scour the aisles and start to wonder if anyone here is lost. It's Valentine's weekend in Aldi, and there are hideous red and pink banners strung up all over the shop. Cut-out hearts dangle over my head as I venture down the middle aisle of wonder. Of one-time hobbies and inflatable paddling pools and big ugly teddy bears with plush hearts that say I LOVE YOU in neat red stitch.

So there I am, eyeing up a pair of sparkly jelly wellies, when I see him. The man upstairs.

It's been so long since I last saw him that I can't help staring. He's shaved his head.

What's his name again? It's an odd one, like him. Begins with a U, I think.

Technically, we used to be neighbours. U lived upstairs in the second of three split maisonettes on our street. But he moved out months ago, apparently. I didn't see him leave.

Careful to keep my distance, I follow him into the frozen section and watch him stockpile lean chicken like there's no tomorrow. He's even musclier now; so muscly that even his veins are trying to pop out of their fleshy prison. Perhaps he thinks this looks good to women. Or perhaps he just thinks it looks good.

I wonder… did he shave his head before or after the woman upstairs left him?

I watch U struggle with his heavy basket. He's overdone

57

it on the chicken fillets. I guess he is still human after all, under all that muscle and pretence.

He used to have a girlfriend. Or, at least, a girl friend. The non-official type, you know?

Anyway, there used to be a young woman – mid-thirties, I reckon – who came to stay with him upstairs. Every Thursday, like clockwork. Sometimes she would spend the whole weekend there. I never saw her, but I heard her, all right. It took me longer than it should have to realise that they weren't building IKEA furniture up there.

Clonk clonk clonk clonk.

I used to get angry about it, what with having to get up for work on a Friday and not being able to sleep and all. But it didn't take long for the knocking to stop and the shouting to start. And somehow, the arguments were so much worse. So I invested in a decent pair of earplugs and took up drinking a nightcap or two. Good, stiff bourbon. And that worked, for a while.

U closes the freezer door and turns his stubbly head my way. I duck into cleaning supplies before he can spot me, hiding behind the multipacks of kitchen roll. I don't think he saw me.

His head really does look awful, shaven like that.

Later that night, I lie awake in bed and stare into the gloom. My eyes trace the outline of sad suits on the clothing rail opposite, all the way along to the tattered black handbag hanging on the end.

My mind begins to wander, as it often does, and I think about seeing U in the supermarket today.

Did he shave off all that lovely brown hair before or after the woman upstairs left him?

I remember it well. It was a Saturday night, and I was minding my own business, eating beans on toast as Anton Du Beke nailed the American Smooth on *Strictly Come Dancing*. I can't stand that show, but I still tune in every week.

The black batons had just started twirling, when it all changed upstairs.

"JUST SHUT UP!" Her, angry. "SHUT UP!"

Smash. A lamp? A plate?

Him, ferocious and stomping across the ceiling. "DON'T YOU TELL ME TO—"

Crash!

Thud.

Then it all went very quiet upstairs. Rapid feet, lighter than his, scurried down the stairs. And the final slam of the front door shook my walls, rattled the dusty bone china.

I didn't bother to go up and see if U was okay – breakups are always nasty business.

Good for her, I thought. Then I smiled, and sliced into my toast as the scores came in on TV.

It's an eight from Craig Revel-Horwood.

Anton deserved nine.

★

Daylight is starting to push through the curtains when there's a confident knock at the door. Irritated, I scrape out of bed and tie myself into a dressing gown, creeping up to the peephole in the door. Just in case it's a serial killer.

A scrawny delivery guy waits in the hallway, clutching a small brown parcel. He looks young and inoffensive.

I open up.

"Morning," he says, avoiding eye contact. "I've got a package for number four, could you sign for it?"

"Number four?" I repeat.

"Yes, madam."

Urgh, *madam*! He's worse than a serial killer.

I examine the parcel, addressed to *Mrs Celia Radcliffe.*

I should probably tell the delivery man that there's been a mistake. That the man upstairs, Mr U-something Radcliffe, moved out ages ago. And there's certainly no Mrs Radcliffe living up there either.

But then again, he called me madam.

"Of course," I smile, squiggling some illegible doodle onto his handheld device. He leaves, as every postie must, and I lock the door and toss the package aside.

As I trudge back to bed, I catch sight of myself in the hallway mirror. It needs polishing.

I look older. When did I get so tired?

Perhaps I need polishing too. A shower might help.

I'm towel drying my dripping hair when there's a loud *bonk* on the ceiling. As if someone has jumped, or dropped something heavy. I freeze and listen.

What if I'm wrong? What if the man upstairs didn't move out? What if someone has broken in?

Suddenly, it seems like the perfect time to hand deliver the mysterious package.

Slipping into a clean white t-shirt and tracksuit bottoms, I march upstairs and bang on the door.

I wait, but no one answers. Whoever's up there, they don't want to see me.

I'm not that scary looking, am I?

Giving up, I go to the house next door and knock for the nosy lady downstairs – the retired one who's always home. I knock again, harder; sometimes the old bat's hard of hearing.

What's her name again? Something beginning with D… Della? Debbie?

Nope. It's long gone.

D opens the door – and I swear she's shrunk again. I ask if she's seen the man upstairs.

"Uter?" D says. "I thought he moved out last year? There was a van outside that came to take away his stuff. Dining chairs and IKEA units and all sorts."

I nod. "That's what I thought. But I also thought I heard someone up there just now."

"Really?" D says. "What, like a burglar?"

"I guess."

"Well, good luck to him," she sniffs. There's relish in her voice, the kind that satisfies a vicious gossip. "From what I saw, he even packed the kitchen sink!"

D is a funny old woman. The totally fearless kind that I have come to appreciate. But I don't laugh. "Oh right," I say. "That's good, then."

"Are you okay, Lisa?" D asks, hand on hip. "You look tired."

I've always thought it's rude when people say that. Backhanded.

Venomous, I smile.

"I'm fine, I just haven't been sleeping well. Must be a change in the weather."

Another pointless thing British people say.

"Oh, I know!" She gobbles it up. "Did you hear that wind last night? It was dreadful. Kept me awake for hours…"

D prattles on, eyes widening as she talks. I tune her out, staring into those mesmerising white cue balls. If it weren't for her freckled skin and her frizz of grey hair and her little duck egg blue cardigan, she'd be quite terrifying.

"…Anyway," D says, "I'd love to stay and chat, but I've got to drop my grandson off at school this morning, so I must go and check on him."

"That's no problem at all."

We exchange goodbyes, and D shuffles back inside. I'm about to make my escape, when a baby's gurgle comes from the top of the stairs.

I look. There's a carrier out on the landing, two tiny blue sock-covered feet kicking. Something deep within me stirs, and I find myself unable to move. Unable to look away. But the longer I stare, the more unsettled I feel.

Then its mother appears and breaks the spell. It's Selma – the nice one who lives with her long-term boyfriend. This must be the sprog she popped out back in March.

Selma notices me as she locks up the flat. "Hello!"

"Hi." I sigh as she descends the stairs, bundle of joy in hand.

The baby is asleep and says nothing. The little cherub only screams at nighttime.

"How are you?" I say, not waiting for an answer. "Did you know that number four moved out?"

Number four. The man upstairs.

"Yes, so I heard," Selma says. She tucks a strand of dyed red hair behind her ear. "Pamela mentioned it a while back."

"Who?"

"Pamela."

I stare at her, blank as a notepad.

"The *older* lady," she prompts, jerking a thumb at D's door. "In number one?"

"Right," I say, frowning. D really doesn't look like a Pamela. "She's nice."

Selma smiles. "She is."

God, what a boring person Selma is. I'd give anything for someone of interest around here. I say, bring the man upstairs back. String up his name in lights like they do on Broadway.

THE MAN UPSTAIRS
FOR ONE NIGHT ONLY!

I could turn my flat into a ticket office, charge people to see him.

One ticket to the freak show, please!

"I'm glad I caught you," Selma says. "I've actually got a letter for you." Popping baby down, she retrieves a plain white envelope from her handbag. "They put it in my letterbox by accident."

"Thanks."

At a glance, I can see it's from Scottish Power.

Good, I think. *I'll introduce that to my shredder later.*

Selma waits for me to say something else. It's a pause almost as pregnant as she was.

"How's baby?" I ask, careful to avoid any names or genders.

And there it is. The glow of a proud new mother, demanding to be indulged.

"Good, thank you," Selma beams. "She's sleeping well."

A girl, then. Poor soul.

"Aww," I say, looking at the baby again. "I bet you're pleased. I'm SO happy for you."

And I mean it, too.

I wish I was sleeping well.

Back in my own block, I check my mailbox in case any other postal blunders have occurred – and the man upstairs' mailbox too, for good measure. I have to wedge my hand right in there to feel around for any sharp envelope corners, but come up disappointed.

I don't know what I was expecting. Confirmation of a psychiatric test? A severed finger?

Any of that would've been better than nothing.

As for me, I have no interest in booking an eye test, or getting 10% off my next order of some body cream I'm never going to buy – I just wanted the free sample, like any other normal human being. I don't want cold letters *'to the occupant'*, or written confirmation to Mrs Imbo that the ground rent has gone up again. That it's going to cost me even more to live in a peeling shoebox in the middle of nowhere; for some sad little man who left his half-baked ambitions in Aldi to come and mow the grass outside the developer show homes, while the spiders weave happy little webs on my front door, hanging from iced threads. I could laugh. I could cry.

But luckily, there's no more mail today.

★

Alone in the dark, I pace around the frosty neighbourhood to kill some time. There's no point trying to sleep – I haven't slept in days – and I can hear my thoughts so much better at night.

I check my phone for the time, the screen light blinding.

It's quarter to two, and I have no messages.

The night air is cold and unforgiving. I should have worn my hat. But I grit my teeth and keep moving.

As I round the corner and trudge back towards home, I see it. My second clue.

The car is back. The horrible, neon green sports car that belongs to the man upstairs. It's parked outside the front of the building, waving at me like a confident toddler.

God, I hate that car.

I fish in my pockets for my house keys, my breath curling into thin white smoke. Fingers clutching cool metal, I look to the sky. Even the stars look dull tonight.

I'm about to head back inside, when the window above my flat fills with warm orange light. Suddenly more moth than human, I gaze up in wonder. I forget the cold. I forget myself.

So, it's true. The man upstairs is back!

Either that, or I'm starting to lose my mind. Seeing things that aren't really there.

Willing myself to pull it together, I go inside and take a bottle of bourbon to bed.

But even as I shiver against the cold duvet, my mind won't stop whirring.

If his girlfriend left him, the moving van took his furniture away, and I am the only one who didn't see him go, what is the man upstairs doing back here? Is the green car really there, or is it a figment of my imagination, a creation of insomnia?

I close my eyes and imagine him. The man upstairs, standing in an empty room. Wondering if he's made a mistake.

If he really isn't there, why did he turn on the light?

★

Sometimes, when I can sleep, I have this recurring dream. A dream that I am a space traveller without a crew. I know I don't belong here. But I put on my white helmet anyway, and climb out into the welcoming arms of darkness.

I float along, weightless. Taking in the majesty of the universe.

But when I return to my ship, the door is sealed shut. I can't get back in. So I feel around in the cushiony pocket of my spacesuit and find a Swiss army knife. That'll do.

With a few quick slices, I cut my cord. The one that ties me to my abandoned ship. And I drift into the silent abyss.

Hours go by. Days. Until finally, a comet in red hot motion sails towards me, burning my retinas.

But I'm not afraid anymore.

I reach out, singe my fingertips. Watch the skin begin to melt down…

I never find out what happens at the end. Something always wakes me.

This time, it's a yell from above.

Bleary-eyed and sweaty, I come to, bedroom objects revealing themselves to me one by one. And I'm angry with the man upstairs, or whoever is up there, hiding.

To keep me up at night is a nuisance. But to wake me from my dreams is unforgivable.

I fling back the duvet, cold air clinging to my skin. Stumbling in the dark, my toes find socks. I pull them on with unburned, reformed fingers, and find the light switch. It's too bright, so I flick it straight back off and feel for my grey hoodie on the back of the door. My stomach is tying itself in knots, over and over. Tighter and tighter. I guess I didn't detach my safety cord after all.

It's now or never. I can't keep living like this.

I exhale and step out into the hallway. Zipping the hoodie, I race up the stairs, triggering the motion detector lights as I hammer on the door to number four.

What do I say?

Realising I haven't thought this through whatsoever – that it's silly o'clock in the morning – I start to panic. What do I do now? When he opens the door, should I complain about the noise? If I ask if everything is okay, will that make him more suspicious of me, listening in? Was the noise that woke me even real?

I slap my cheeks. Of course it was real.

I have nothing to fear, nothing to hide. But the man upstairs has a secret.

My heart in my mouth, I rap on the door again. But still, there's no answer.

What's keeping him? Must I be awake, for the man upstairs to sleep? Like sun and moon. One must be up, while the other is down.

No, enough. This has to end.

I take a breath and force open the door, expecting to hit a chain, a lock – anything to keep burglars and unwanted neighbours out. Instead, I stumble into the flat and stand alone in a silent dark strip of hallway.

"Hello?" I say into the void.

The low wind whistles outside. My clammy hands twitch, wishing they had a weapon in them. Just in case.

I edge into the living room and switch on the light. It's empty. All the furniture is gone, just like D and Selma said.

Swivelling to face the kitchen, I see there are no red digits on the oven clock. I open the fridge. There's no food, no light. Everything is switched off.

"It's me," I say to the room, in case the man upstairs is watching me from a dark corner. Waiting to jump out. "Your neighbour. From downstairs?"

He's hiding. He has to be.

Where is he?

Repressing a shudder, I back out into the hallway and throw open the bathroom door.

There's a toilet, sink basin, shower. But no shower gel, or towels on the rack, or loo roll on the holder. There isn't even a toothbrush. It's all so… pristine.

The swinging white light cord is the only sign of life.

Staggering back out into the hallway, I wipe the sweat from my forehead and lock eyes with the bedroom door.

This is the last room. He has to be here.

Taking one last, deep breath, I put on my space helmet. And then I step into the unknown.

The harsh yellow-white light of the hallway shines into the dark bedroom. I see a bed frame, but no mattress or pillows. A nightstand, but no lamp. And no curtains on the window. I squint outside and see that the toxic green car is missing.

Suddenly, it's all too much.

I sink to the floor, gripping tufts of stiff, cream carpet between my fingers, wishing I could rip them out. But in my sorrow, there is also relief. Something in me lifts.

He's gone. The man upstairs is gone.

I laugh through my tears. Lie down in a pool of moonlight. And finally, my eyes close.

★

Something touches my shoulder, and I judder awake.

"Hello?" says a soft, cautious voice.

I rub my heavy eyes, painfully aware of the sun's rays. Then I look to the stranger.

It isn't the man upstairs, but a doe-eyed young woman looking down on me. Fear, mingled with curiosity. Who am I? And what am I doing in her flat?

But she doesn't run from me. She crouches down and asks if I'm okay.

I want to scream. But my throat is dry, and composure is so hard to come by these days.

"You must be Celia," I manage.

She nods, a smile playing at her lips. It dawns on me how very pretty she is, and my eyes brim with tears as I realise that I am definitely not okay, and I can't hide anymore.

So, I tell her everything, the words spilling out quicker than I can stop them. My body trembles as I recall the endless fights with my husband. The long nights I spent chained to my desk, closing deals. And for what? More money? Sure, we enjoyed some flashy couple's holidays, fuelled by sunshine and sea and late-night lovemaking after a few too many mojitos. But somehow, I was never there when it really mattered. The arguments became daily routine. I worked later at the office to avoid them. Started to miss birthdays. Christenings. Cheap wine dinner parties with friends. I'd come home exhausted and collapse into the armchair. My husband was always asleep by then, and never pleased to see me if I woke him. We performed this sad play for months, like two ghosts silently haunting the same house.

But on Saturday nights, we took off our angry masks.

We always sat down to watch *Strictly* together, because my husband liked it. We'd crack open a bottle of wine and discuss the dances.

Look at that frame! He must have had dance lessons before. Stiff as board – she's got to go!

I was born with two left feet, my husband little better. But after a few glasses of Merlot, he'd get up to demonstrate the "proper" Tango technique. He'd pull me from the sofa and twirl me around and dip me to the floor until I screamed with laughter – almost dropping me in the process. We were 'us' again, just for the night. It was enough.

Everything changed when my mother-in-law died. I took the day off work for the funeral and told my husband I was sorry, and held his hand through the ceremony and the sandwich buffet. But that experience changed his mind about a lot of things. Flipped a switch in his brain. Grief does that to people, I think. My husband got angry. He knew that I didn't particularly care about my job, as long as the money was coming in. He couldn't understand why I was wasting my life. Why I was avoiding him. Was I bothering to come home for dinner tonight? Did I even want children?

Of course I did. But it was never the right time. My accounts were my babies, growing bigger and more demanding each day. And my husband hated being stuck at home, job hunting. I know he did. Every interview "went well". And all I could do was say sorry when he didn't get the job. Over and over again. I was scared of losing the man I loved. Scared of being alone.

So, one day, I flicked a brain switch of my own. I spoke up to my boss, tried to be braver about leaving on time. I stopped working late altogether. But sadly, my "dwindling commitment to this company" did not go unnoticed. I made a choice. I thanked my boss for his time, and quit that same morning.

My husband would find another job, and so would I. We'd start trying for a family again. I had enough in the bank to balance the books for a few months, maybe take us away for a nice weekend in London. It was time to start living again!

I rushed home from the office, grinning from ear to ear. Passing strangers stared at me as if I were a madwoman, but I didn't care. I ran all the way home from the train station in my tights, high heels in hand. Burst through the kitchen door, ecstatic to share my news. Expecting to see my husband standing there, stirring his morning coffee, or pulling a load of wet washing from the machine.

But I found the kitchen empty.

I called his name. Checked every room. I even looked in the storage cupboards, where I noticed that one of the suitcases was missing. I didn't think anything of it, until I saw that his slippers were gone. He never went anywhere without his slippers.

I was too late.

Wiping my tears on toilet paper, I saw his forgotten blue toothbrush on the bathroom sink. Still in the pot, beside my red. The one he would never come back for.

I finish telling my story to Celia, and sit quietly until my body stops shaking, my eyes raw.

She waits.

"You live here, don't you?" I eventually ask her. "In this flat?"

"I used to."

"Why did you leave him?"

"Leave him?" This amuses her. "Is that what my husband told you?"

"No… I just assumed… I…"

Apparently exhausted from recalling my past, words fail me now. Celia is patient as I try to put the puzzle pieces together. Perhaps I've got this all muddled up. Perhaps the man upstairs was the one who left, and the green car belongs to Celia. And when did they get married?

None of it makes any sense. My head is pounding.

"I don't understand," I tell her. "You're so lovely. How could your husband leave you?"

This woman should slap me, should call the police to report that a wild, inconsolable stranger has broken into her home. But she doesn't.

She laughs.

"Well, obviously I'd prefer that my husband didn't have to leave," Celia says. "But I don't think Uter's work would like that very much. And besides, at least one of us has to get the new house ready."

"New house?"

Her hands glide down to her belly, and only now do I see the small bump there. The promise of new life and love. I feel so stupid. So worthless.

"So, you did move out?" I say, thick as custard.

"Yes," Celia says. "I just came by to pick up the mail. I haven't got around to redirecting it all to our new address yet, you see."

The mail! I want to burst into tears again.

"What day is it today?" I ask.

"Saturday."

"Oh. Right."

I don't know what to do with that information. I don't know why I asked.

A frown sneaks past Celia's smile. "Shall we… get you home now then?"

I nod, pressing my lips together to stop them from shaking.

"All right then."

Celia offers me her arm, which I take, and together we make our way out of the flat and back down the stairs. She walks me all the way back to my living room, and helps me down into the armchair. I've always hated the armchair. My husband chose it.

"Can I get you anything?" Celia asks. She looks a little concerned. "Tea? Coffee?"

"Bourbon," I say. "In the cupboard, where the glasses are."

She looks concerned, but fetches the bottle and free-pours a measure. It's far too much, but I don't complain. Pregnancy aside, it's clear that she isn't a whisky drinker.

"Perfect," I say. "Thank you."

"Are you sure you're going to be okay?" she asks.

I'm not. So I ask her the time instead.

"Ten thirty," she says.

I nod, considering that.

"Okay then, Mrs Imbo," Celia says, patting my hand. "You take care now."

I don't bother to watch her go, I just wait to hear the click of the door latch. I am used to it now. Somehow, it hurts less when you don't see these things happen.

As I stare at the television, switched off, I catch my reflection. A single tear rolls down my cheek.

I drain the bourbon. Not long until *Strictly*.

★★★

Becky Leeson is a 27-year-old author from Buckinghamshire. 'The Man Upstairs' is her debut short story, inspired by the isolation many of us experienced in lockdown.

Becky is also writing her first YA dystopian sci-fi novel.

When she isn't hammering a keyboard, Becky enjoys cooking and classic rock music. It's nice and loud, so the neighbours can enjoy it too.

Twitter/Instagram: @bookyleeson

WAITING TO BE LOVED

Allie Atkinson

This is it. She'd been waiting for this night since the invite had popped up in her inbox two months before. The Company Annual Ball. Every detail had been meticulously planned from that very moment. There were daily visualisations of the black gown with a sweetheart neckline and diamante belt resting just below the bust. Beneath the dress, she wore a delicate pair of black four-inch sandals to create femininity and reveal just a glimpse of her painted toenails as she moved. Baby blue, of course, and they matched the blue lilies that added a unique accent to her French manicured fingernails. Around her neck rested a thin, silver chain with a petite heart pendant for subtle extra sparkle. Her make-up was natural and soft, and her strawberry-blonde hair had been professionally styled into a neat up-do. Lottie had seen herself standing in this exact spot a thousand times. The large oak doors with their worn brass handles that would be cold to touch. The bright lights and live music that would envelop her as she moved into the ballroom. Her hand was sure to need the mahogany handrail for balance as she took each of the stone steps slowly and deliberately. One. Two. Three…

And that's when it would happen. Someone would spot her. It didn't matter who. In fact, the person's identity changed every time she visualised it, but someone, somewhere in the room would notice her. They would notice her in a way she'd never been noticed before. Gradually, the room would fall silent as each set of eyes came to rest on her. Lottie's Cinderella moment.

Then he would look up. He would pretend not to notice her at first, of course, to avoid drawing any attention. But it would wash over him like a wave of desire and the penny would finally drop. She was suddenly no longer the woman he wanted to keep hidden away from others or a woman he saw no future with. She was now all he could see in his future. And he wanted others to know, to understand that she was his, and only his.

But as Lottie stood at the doors now, the stark reality of what was about to happen pierced through her fantasy. Sure, she had the dress, the shoes, the make-up and the up-do. The doors were the same and she could already hear the loud music. None of that would be a disappointment. But Lottie knew that no one was going to spot her. There would be no Cinderella moment. No realisation of true love by the man she'd been secretly seeing for almost a year. No, this entrance would be no different to any other entrance she had experienced. Lottie wasn't born to stand out in a crowd. She wasn't sure she'd been born to stand out enough for *one* person to notice her, let alone everyone in the room.

Nevertheless, she opened the doors and made her way to the stone steps. She held the handrail and looked out across the room at the sea of people she knew so well. There were all the familiar faces that she spent the majority of her life around, yet never outside of work, except for the annual ball.

★

Staring at the floor, listening to the same tiresome conversations he had heard just an hour before in the office, Connor couldn't help but wonder why on earth he had agreed to attend the company ball. A night spent with people he had just been with all day, and who complained endlessly about work but spoke about nothing else, was not really his scene. Connor wasn't a formal, suit and tie kind of guy. He was much more of the 'jeans and tee shirt whilst binge watching the latest hit television series' kind to be honest. But despite being completely out of his comfort zone, Connor had rooted out his navy pin-striped trousers with matching waistcoat and paired them with his cream shirt and brown shoes. It wasn't the polished grey look that most of the men had gone for, but he had known he was a little bit of an outsider from starting at the company a few months earlier. It didn't faze him.

Finally, the conversation was coming to a familiar conclusion, and Connor lifted his head to rejoin the celebrations. As he nonchalantly looked around the room, his eyes were drawn to the large oak doors. They had stopped on those doors a couple of times already as he'd waited. Anticipated. But this time was different.

This time, she was there, standing at the top of the steps, and Connor immediately recognised the thumping feeling in his chest and the hot, clammy sensation in his hands. Lottie always had this effect on him, but tonight... tonight she simply took his breath away.

That was the reason he had chosen to attend. Not to be sociable. Not to have meaningless, repetitive conversations with people he barely knew. It was Lottie. She was the reason. The woman he had secretly admired from afar.

★

Lottie surveyed the crowd, looking for a connection, an invitation for her to join them, but as predicted, no one had noticed she was there. So, taking a deep breath, Lottie began to take the first few steps down before she stopped abruptly.

Her breath caught. Her chest tightened. Her cheeks burned and her body trembled as she tried to make sense of what she was seeing. She squeezed her eyes shut quickly to make it all stop and go away, before bravely opening them again. Slowly, she began to process the scene that was playing out before her.

He was there, standing just beyond the first group of people. The suit she had collected from the dry cleaners that afternoon looked perfectly smooth on him now, matched with a slim white shirt, grey tie, and black polished shoes. His dark hair was typically styled into a small flick across to the left. Lottie preferred it without the wax, as nature intended. It was softer and kinder, the real him, she had thought. Although, right now, she wasn't sure that was the real him at all. Taking a moment to gather herself, she moved her attention to the lady standing next to him, or more specifically, to the lady's hand that was gently interlocked with his.

The nausea consumed Lottie and she was sure the colour had drained from her face for everyone to see. Her heart pounded so hard, the vibrations could be felt in her ears and her mind desperately tried to make sense of what was happening. She didn't understand. How… When did… Why didn't he…? The beginnings of so many questions whirled around her head as she watched them gaze at each other lovingly. The lady swept her long auburn hair over her shoulder to rest down the back of the red, lace cocktail dress she was effortlessly showcasing. There was no question as to whether she would be noticed on arrival. How could Lottie compete with that?

And it was at that moment that Lottie knew the ball was over for her this year. No one would know. No one had realised she was even there yet. She lowered her head, turned on her heels and made her way back to the oak doors as quickly as possible.

It wasn't until she reached her sofa, away from the possibility of anyone seeing her, that Lottie allowed the full load of the evening to be realised. There were so many tears for him, for the future she thought could have been, but mainly for her. For allowing herself to believe she could be enough for him, and for not accepting that it was never going to be that way. But it was also deeper than just tonight. She cried out of fear that it would always be this way. What if she really wasn't enough for anyone? What if no one ever thought she was worth loving completely and unconditionally? And it was those questions that Lottie was desperately trying to answer as she cried herself to sleep.

★

A gentle tapping noise brought Lottie back into her living room. She stared at the pink and grey flowers on the wallpaper behind her television, unsure whether she had really heard the sound or dreamt it. But there it was again. It wasn't a knock she recognised, so it couldn't be her parents or her best friend. This knock was rhythmed and upbeat and, somehow, masculine, if you could say that about a door knock. It sounded again, a little louder and more urgent this time. Lottie's stomach dropped to the floor as the possibility that *he* could be knocking crossed her mind. 'Why would it be him?' she questioned, before deciding it definitely wasn't his knock either. Again it sounded as Lottie slid herself from the sofa, stretched and dragged her feet to the door.

'Connor?!' Lottie was aware of the shock and confusion in her voice.

'Good Morning! I thought you might be wanting one of these,' he said, handing her a takeaway coffee cup. 'And maybe a walk in the beautiful sunshine?' he added with a gentle smile.

Perhaps it was the way the light was lying across his face, but Lottie suddenly realised how warm Connor's smile was. His appearance matched what Lottie knew of his personality at work – quite relaxed and mellow. And although he was only in his early thirties like Lottie, he had a reputation for being calm in stressful situations, the type of calmness you only develop through experience. But it was the way that Connor's thin lips brightened his whole face when he smiled to create little dimples in his cheeks that captured Lottie on her doorstep. And the way it drew attention to his distinctive blue eyes. Lottie had noticed those. Practically everyone had, but she suddenly felt like she had never taken the time to really look at him besides a passing glance as they crossed each other in the staff room. He definitely wasn't your typical 'good-looking' man, but there was something about him, she thought.

He made his way into her living room, which looked rather small with his six foot two, slender silhouette now standing in the centre of it. Lottie paused as she watched him, still confused as to why Connor was in her flat with coffee in the first place. She was about to ask, but Connor spoke first.

'I don't mind waiting whilst you get changed,' he said, gesturing towards the ball gown she was still wearing from the night before.

'Right. Erm, okay, I will be back in a minute,' Lottie replied as she made her way to the bedroom.

She closed the door behind her and took a deep breath before sipping her coffee. It was *her* coffee. Actually *her* coffee. Not just a standard white coffee, but the cortado coffee with skimmed milk she ordered herself every morning. The coffee no one else could remember the name of. How did Connor know? They didn't even work in the same department. Now even more confused, Lottie changed into her denim shorts and white 'be kind' tee shirt. She relaxed her hair to rest on her shoulders and removed the tear-stained remains of last night's make-up. It all felt so pointless and pathetic now. Make-up and hair were never going to convince someone to fall in love with her. She popped her hair into a messy bun and added a little blusher to her cheeks, before finishing her coffee and slipping on her white trainers.

'Let's go for a walk with Connor,' she said wearily to herself in the mirror.

They walked in silence. An awkward silence that made Lottie feel quite uncomfortable. But she wasn't sure what to say to break it. She wasn't even sure why they were doing this. Should she ask? Maybe not, she didn't want to sound rude after he had gone to the effort of bringing her coffee first thing. Staring straight out ahead of her, wrapped up in her own thoughts, Lottie had not noticed the subtle glances from Connor or the way he dropped his head and smiled to himself after each one. She was also oblivious to the little signs of nervousness he was displaying; the almost-said questions that he just couldn't seem to vocalise and the quick run of his fingers through his curly hair after each failed attempt. Connor had been waiting to spend a morning with Lottie from the first moment he had seen her, but he knew the timing was not right. In truth, he wasn't sure the timing was right now either, but he couldn't not see her, not after last night. He cringed slightly thinking about the pain and humiliation that was written all over

Lottie's face as she stood on the stairs of the ballroom. He had wanted to run to her, to hold her and tell her how stunning he thought she looked. In fact, he had begun to make his excuses to those around him, but before he could make his way across the room, she had gone. Connor left shortly after that too.

As the pair approached a set of large iron gates, Lottie realised they were about to enter the same park where she spent most of her lunch breaks. She was completely unaware that they had walked that far but she breathed a sigh of relief to know they had. It was her peaceful place for when everything felt too much. Somewhere to stop and ground herself amongst the fresh air and calming influence of nature in a bustling concrete jungle.

'I walk in this park all the time. I love it!' she shared with Connor, who gently smiled and nodded.

'Have you been here before?' she asked.

'I come here occasionally. The wooded area is my favourite.' He gestured to a smaller path that led off into a much denser area that Lottie couldn't recall walking through before.

'Why not?' she replied with a shrug of her shoulders.

The path was barely visible amongst the bushes and trees that surrounded it. The whole area was full of life and vibrant autumn colours, and yet it was calm and tranquil. Lottie's breath caught as she felt the full impact of her surroundings. She paused and closed her eyes as she absorbed the atmosphere. Birds chirping away to themselves, trees gently rustling in the breeze, and the crunching of leaves under Connor's feet as he continued to walk along the path ahead. And somewhere faintly in the background, there was the slight hum and whooshing of the busy main road that they had just walked along. How strange to compare the two environments that were so close together. Lottie wasn't sure why, but she felt like she wanted to smile. A deep, soulful smile.

'Are you okay?'

Connor's voice cut through the quiet. Lottie opened her eyes and nodded before catching up with him. The sounds. The colours. The smells. It all felt magical and Lottie couldn't bear the idea of returning to the noise just yet. They weaved around the trunks and branches, until they reached a small bench. It was a very simple bench with two legs and a plank across the top, but she sensed it held a lot of history. Branches from the surrounding plants and bushes tangled their way around it, inviting it to be part of the natural habitat and Lottie couldn't help but wonder how many people had sat on that bench thinking to themselves, calming themselves, or maybe even finding themselves.

Without saying a word, they each took a seat and stared into the plantation ahead. Once again, Connor stole a few moments to study Lottie. Her eyes looked sore and tired, probably from crying the night before he assumed. Why couldn't she see what he could see? It frustrated Connor that Lottie longed to be loved by those who couldn't appreciate her true worth. Those who fed their own ego by bringing others down. He would never treat her that way. He would never treat anyone that way. But Lottie… Lottie was more special than she would ever know.

'What's your favourite tree? You know, the one you find yourself staring at all the time?' Lottie asked, stopping his train of thought.

'Erm…' he stuttered trying to digest the question, before realising he knew exactly what his answer should be. 'The tree over there on the ground.' He pointed to a large, broken trunk that lay covered by other shrubbery. You could almost imagine the storm it must have experienced to create such damage. But to Connor, the damage was part of its charm. It had been battered and beaten in the past, but it was still there supporting others, providing a habitat for all kinds of wildlife and a playground for young children.

'What?!' Lottie half laughed thinking she must have misheard. 'It's completely collapsed and overwhelmed by everything going on around it!'

'But it is still the most beautiful one here to me,' Connor replied confidently, no longer looking at the tree but at Lottie instead.

And, for the first time, Lottie was looking back at him too.

★★★

Originally from Dagenham, Essex, Allie lives in Leicestershire with her husband, Chris, and is a stay-at-home mummy to their three children. In 2020, Allie co-authored the *Love Thy Body Project – Real Life Stories: Volume One*, which became an Amazon bestseller in ebook and paperback. Since then, she has launched her own blog, 'Just One Mama', sharing her thoughts and feelings on some of her motherhood experiences, alongside wonderful guest writers, in the hope of providing support, comfort and inspiration to other parents experiencing something similar.

Her blog can be followed at:

www.justonemama.co.uk

And Allie can be reached on Instagram:

www.instagram.com/just.one.mama

Or Facebook:

www.facebook.com/justonemama

Or Twitter:

www.twitter.com/JustOneMama1

LIGHTS, CAMERA, CHOCOLATE

Holly Philpott

"So, we'd like to offer you the role. Would you like to accept this?"

You know those moments in life, when everything seems to be plodding along and nothing really seems to happen, like a pause – then that pause ends, and your life becomes *changed forever*? I think that's happening to me, right here in my university room, on my chair with the pom-pom cushions.

"Of course! Seriously, thank you somuchfortheopportunity," I stammer over my words, which is not down to me being nervous but rather that I've already had two coffees today, and it's only midday. "You won't regret this; I'll learn so much about the camera setup and assist the directors on set—"

"Oh… I forgot to mention that part. Your role is not in media production, which I understand is what you signed up for, but when you came to the interview our team loved your enthusiasm. We knew we wanted you on set but as we had too many people in the media sector, we've decided to offer you the role of one of the two main lead actors in the advert.

Acting? I'd sent in an application to be part of the media team for a TV advert that was shooting in our area a few weeks ago, as part of my media portfolio at university. The advert would be for the chocolate brand, Temptations, to showcase their new range of luxury chocolate boxes; it was a brand I'd loved for years, buying sharing boxes to eat to myself while watching a film (no, I'm definitely not greedy), and they were always the best chocolates to munch at Christmas, when you feel like a snow globe and chocolates are the only thing you could possibly eat a hundred of. Yet somehow, in a twist of fate – chocolatey fate – I was going to be an actress? I'd never done acting, never been serious enough to consider it… could I really do it?

Think of the opportunity, a voice whispered loudly in my head. That was true. And, a bit louder: *Think of the free chocolates*. That was very true.

"Have you cast the other lead? You said there were two," I say into the phone, trying to think of local actors who could've auditioned.

"Yes, we have – his name's Russell Jones, you may have heard of him. So, do you accept the role? I know it isn't what you thought it'd be…" Russell Jones, the famous actor? He's only a few years older than me, and one of the best young actors in the industry. He also seems lovely; after seeing him in some comedy adverts and his first major role on TV, he comes across as funny, charming and (not that I have a celebrity crush or anything) classically handsome. *Think of Russell Jones.*

"Yes. I'll do it," I say, smiling and screaming on the inside. Me, Ally, an actress for a TV advert?! And with Russell... I can't wait.

"Hiya!" I'm beaming from ear to ear as I stand in front of Russell, taking in his reddish-brown hair and black jeans/ t-shirt combo. It's the day of the TV advert shoot, and as we only have today to make things perfect because of the company budgets, I want to get off to the right start. Every inch of my body is bursting with happiness, which explains why my normally frizzy blonde hair is now bouncy and shiny. Or is that the new hair mask I used? Either way, my mood is at an all-time high, like I'm on the highest point of a roller coaster and adrenaline is pumping through my veins; the ride over the top and round the rest of the roller coaster is going to be incredible. Russell looks at me and, to my surprise, not one glimmer of a smile settles on his face.

"Hi." It's curt and blunt and, although it's not a huge deal, my heart beats a little bit faster than before, as though my need to appear cool in front of this incredible actor is switched on and warming up. Instead of going forward, the roller coaster is falling backwards, down the hill, and making me feel a bit queasy.

"So... exciting, right? Me, you, in an advert – I've never done this before but I can't wait." Plastering a smile back on my face to cover up the panic, I look up at Russell but he's already turning away from me.

"Well, good luck. I've done this before, so I don't need luck, but have a nice time." And with that, Russell walks away. We're standing near a bus stop, where the first scene of the advert is being shot. Our characters are shy and see each other on the bus, glancing at each other longingly like how I look at a bar of chocolate – completely smitten (it's perfectly normal to love chocolate like that… right?) – and realise they live on the same university block of flats as they walk up the stairs to their accommodation. The girl is visited by the boy the following day in a twist of pure, lovely, chocolatey magic, as from his hands he offers her a Temptations chocolate box. They stand in the girl's university room doorway, getting to know each other – note to self, play Russell the song 'Getting to Know You' later, perhaps it'll cheer him up. Somehow, though, I think a lot of magic from the chocolate gods are needed, if Russell and I are to even get any tingle of chemistry.

Help…

"Okay, Ally, so you're going to walk onto the bus, head down and shy, hunched in shoulders – however best you think a shy person would act. Then you'll look up and spot Russell, and he'll do the same, and you'll just smile at each other. Then you can sit down, and we can end the scene," one of the directors says, and gestures towards the cameras, which flash bright white and red like a warning, or a siren.

"These cameras are rolling as of now, so whenever you're ready." *Okay*, I think this through in my head. *I can do this! Who cares what Russell thinks?* I say to myself as I walk to the bus stop, trying to hide my smile at starting my acting debut. *Who cares what anybody on this bus thinks? I can– can't do this…*

It happens like a flash of lightning, quick and almost unnoticeable. I trip on the step but, as though it's a comedy where everything seems to go wrong for no reason, I fall onto the faded bus floor, feeling the stare of the other actors. Including Russell. I don't even need to look up to tell that he's angry; he's raging, his emotions radiating across the bus in fury. And I'm directly in the target zone. I've messed up twice in front of him now, what's he going to think of me?

"I– I'm so sorry," I say loudly, feeling a bruise form on my knee, like a reminder, as I stand up. Maybe it's not even just my knee that's bruised – my pride feels hurt too, embarrassed, and even though nobody's laughing, I can picture them trying not to. I don't even turn to Russell, knowing that he's staring at my back as I jump out of the bus and go to the toilets nearby, tears pricking my eyes.

After I've left the toilets, I'm being carted away to the university steps, with a dozen crew members swirling around me, bumping into me, talking all around me so their thoughts bleed into one, telling me we've run out of time on the bus for now. Shame creeps onto my face.

"Do you realise there's only one day to film?" I jump and turn to see Russell behind me, arms crossed as he catches up with me. "Don't you learn at university that you need to be professional? I learned that at drama school, haven't you?" He's not wrong – I know we have limited time and it's running out, and with every second that ticks by I feel more and more panicked. But professional? Surely you need to have fun too whilst working on a project like this? Russell needs to calm down, but I don't say anything – why would I? He's a volcano, rage bubbling below the surface. It's not going to be down to me to make him erupt.

"Russell! Ally!" The casting director beckons us over to the stairs, next to the camera crew who have just finished setting up the angles. The stairs look safe enough, pain-free, not somewhere I could trip up easily unlike the bus. There's even a handrail! A handrail! It seems simple enough, but that security is exactly what I need for this next shot.

"All you'll need to do is walk up the stairs, from different directions, and smile at each other as Russell holds the door open for you." As I sneak a glance at Russell, I notice that he nods and is smiling, but when he spots me looking at him, a frown takes its place. Despite the frostiness, it's clear that Russell's a great actor; just like that, he can switch off certain emotions. The smile freezes on my face, but my eyes widen with anxiety. The cameras are on, yet Russell's coldness towards me chills my body to the point where my hands begin to tremble uncontrollably. My heart beats faster as I walk up the steps before Russell and, as our eyes meet, I smile as warmly as I can. He smiles back, playing the shy university student perfectly, professionally. Maybe now he's seen me act without messing up, he'll be happier to have me here—

Or not.

A student is coming towards the door without realising we're filming, and just as I step next to it, he swings it open, not seeing me. The glass window on the door makes a knocking noise as it hits me, its weight heavy and solid against my cheeks.

"Oh!" It turns out that the stairs are deceiving. They seem to move or shift as I recoil from the shock, letting me step out too far and I fall down, down, down to the bottom of the stairs, regaining balance like a child learning to walk.

Great.

My head is woolly, as though it's stuffed with wool, and it's been hit or knocked many times, too many times to count. If shame was a small feeling pulsing through me, it's taken over now, running in my blood and colouring my cheeks a bright, unpleasant red. *Boom-boom, boom-boom, boom-boom* is the rhythm of my heart, the song of today, and there have been too many sad parts to count. The only positive of the day is that I get paid – and get a free box of Temptations chocolates. The crew smile knowingly, say it's all right when I apologise a hundred times, but I can tell that they know they've made a mistake.

I've ruined this for everyone.

"Right… okay, we've only got an hour left of filming time, although I don't know if this is enough time to reshoot what we've made a few errors on." The director avoids my gaze when he says this, which I'm grateful for – but Russell makes up for that by looking at me with contempt.

"So, Ally, all you need to do is sit down on your chair in the room and pretend to do some work. That's all you have to do. Can you do it?" the director asks and I nod silently, knowing that if I mess this up, it's game over for the advert. If I mess up, the team is going to hate me for wasting so much time. If I mess up... Russell's never going to get over it. Sitting in a chair isn't that difficult, right? Knowing how I've been today, maybe it *is*.

Finally, I'm alone, with the cameras in place, the crew working on the rest of the setup, and me waiting, sitting down at the desk, book in hand and staring passively out of the window. The world seems peaceful, the birds flying around in the velvety dark sky, and other little windows from blocks of flats are lit up from within, looking like fairy lights against the night. That's how I should've been today.

The drawer in the desk is slightly ajar and, inside it, I can see some kind of silver glimmer; could it be a notebook, a box? I slide the drawer open quietly and see the one thing that could calm me down after today.

A Temptations chocolate box.

I pull the box out and open it, looking at all of the chocolates as though I've found the biggest jewel in the world. I grin and take one of the truffles and pop it in my mouth. The smooth chocolate shell melts on my tongue, unleashing a liquid filling that's pure, sweet gold. Next, a caramel one, just as rich and lightly salted. And it's while I'm there, allowing the caramel to overwhelm my sense, that I realise this isn't right. I shouldn't be here anymore, not in a world where my co-worker didn't even give me a chance from the first time I said 'hello'. I don't belong... but that's okay. It's really okay.

There's a knock at the door and I hesitantly open it to find Russell there, arms folded, shoulders hunched in together.

"Look, I just needed to tell you that you have to get this right. I—"

"No, I just need to tell you that I'm done. I've had enough of being in a crew where you don't believe in me, and yes, I have really, *really* screwed up today." I laugh awkwardly. "But I have tried to get along with you, have some fun, and have what was meant to be a great day. I guess I was wrong. Tell the crew I'm leaving and that I'm giving up my pay for them to book another day's filming." Russell steps to the side, his expression unreadable, and watches on as I walk down the corridor. "Oh, and Russell—" I stop and turn around, looking him directly in the eyes— "I'm sorry for not being professional enough for you." And as I walk down the long corridor, as tears form once more, as Russell calls my name behind me, I smile.

★

Two weeks later, I'm alone in my room, working on a task my lecturer has set for us, yet my mind drifts back to the advert unconsciously, like I'm in a dream that I can't wake up from. Although unlike a dream, which envelopes you with happiness, this feels like a nightmare. Russell glaring at me. Tripping over on the bus. Feeling the weight of the glass door as it hit my face. All of it. I can't seem to escape.

KNOCK KNOCK.

I slide back away from my desk to open the door, confused because it's a Saturday, and there's normally nobody in on a— Russell?!

He's standing there, chestnut brown hair falling into

his eyes from the blustery winds outside, and in his hands is a box. A 'For the Special Ones' chocolate box from Temptations. I'm inclined to ask questions, but he holds the box out like a peace offering, and I tentatively take a hold of it, glancing back up into Russell's eyes. What's going on?

"I—"

"Before you say anything, I have to show you this." This doesn't seem like the Russell I met a fortnight ago; he's stumbling over his words and as soon as the chocolate box is out of his hands, he's fidgeting frantically. I open my mouth to say something, anything, but he holds a finger up and pulls his phone out of his pocket. There's a video loaded on it, and I instantly recognise the red double-decker bus beside a Temptations chocolate shop. There are fairy lights twinkling in the shop window like stars in the sky, and inside the bus passengers are sitting down. All but one. The only girl standing up has long, curly blonde hair and a baby pink skater skirt on.

Is this the advert? It can't be, because everything went wrong… and that's exactly what happens in the video. My stomach churns as I watch myself fall onto the bus floor, remembering my leg knocking against the step. Why would Russell show me this, when all it makes me feel like doing is crying again? Redder and redder, my cheeks blush as I see the glass door open onto my face. I don't understand… Why am I being shown all of my mistakes that were caught on camera, with sad music in the background? Is this meant to be some kind of punishment? My hand tingles with the urge to slam the door in Russell's face but, somehow, I can't do it. I'm hypnotised by the video. It's as if the glass door's here in front of me and my face hurts as though it's just struck it and tears sting my eyes and—

Wait.

All of a sudden, the video cuts to me in the university dorm, that single camera aimed towards the wooden desk, and I see myself, worn out, exhausted and angry, walking onto the screen and collapsing into the chair, finding the chocolates in the drawer. It seems like, when I thought I was alone, the cameras caught every moment; I must've missed those tell-tale flashing lights on the lenses. My face relaxes on the advert and somehow the editors have managed to focus on the box in my hands. The final image is of me in the chair, eating another chocolate and smiling at the taste of caramel in my mouth, and the words 'Temptations… when life gets you down, all you need is chocolate' are said on a voiceover. The logo for the company swirls around the top of the screen above my head, floating off and then the video comes to a halt.

"What *is* this?" is all I can manage to make my mouth say, and Russell has a small smile across his face.

"This is the Temptations TV advert, with you as the star. I know what you're thinking," he says before I get the chance to interrupt (typical Russell). "But the directors and producers looked back over the footage from the day and noticed that the camera had been rolling when you sat in the university room, eating the chocolates. So, instead of reshooting, they've made the advert to focus around a girl – you – who's having the worst day imaginable, but a box of Temptations chocolates is enough to sweeten life up again.

Please say you're okay with this… the producers had no idea that the day would go so badly, but it ended up giving us a golden advert." My friends would describe me as the chatty one, yet right now in the doorway, with Russell in front of me and the biggest revelation being pushed towards me, I'm well and truly speechless. There are so many thoughts running through my mind, but they're all connected like a web. I can't sift through it all to speak properly.

"I…"

"Please say yes. Please, I feel… I feel terrible after the way I treated you. I take my jobs very seriously – but you know that, after two weeks ago." He chuckles awkwardly. "But you didn't deserve my attitude. I just didn't want to let the team down and so I tried to be professional, but instead I froze you out and made you feel bad. As my little sister would say, I went all Elsa on you." Another chuckle. Could I say yes? Could my embarrassing self be enough for a chocolate advert?

"What about you? You were meant to play a main role."

"Don't worry about that, the company's offered me a job for a few months down the line. You'll see me on your screen soon enough, don't you worry." He's funny. Russell's got a *sense of humour*?! Instead of freezing up around him again, I feel myself thawing, smiling back.

"You know what? Yes! This can be the advert, and I can't wait to see it on TV. I'll email the directors to say thanks. Thank you, Russell. For the chocolates, the advert… it means a lot." We smile at each other for what seems like an eternity but the spell's broken by Russell clearing his throat.

"I, um, was wondering if you wanted to go for a coffee? That is, if you're free? I want to introduce myself properly, apologise a billion times for the way I behaved and, of course, have an amazing mocha with you." Suddenly, I know who Russell is. He comes across as Jack Frost, frosty and stern, but underneath he's kind, funny, even the kind of guy who isn't afraid to admit he's wrong, just so he can start over. Maybe there's more to him than I thought.

"Sure, I'd like that." I take my bag and place the chocolates in there for us to eat as I shut my door (without my face being hit, of course) and walk down the corridor with Russell, grinning when I see some other students stare at us as we pass the kitchen.

I think it's true, what the advert said. When life gets you down, all you need is chocolate... and, if you're lucky, a famous actor friend to eat them with.

★★★

Holly Philpott lives in Leicestershire, where she's currently studying A Levels and dreaming about the future. She's enjoyed writing ever since an English project in primary school, when she had to write a short fantasy story. While she's improved at fiction since her fourteen-paged mermaid tale, the love for writing has never disappeared, and she hopes to continue writing in the future. This is her first published short story and it's been amazing to see everything come together!

JUMPER

Jamie Lewis

Ronnie walked through the harvest-ready cornfield. Her rough outstretched hands brushed against the husks of large plentiful corn, their silky caress tickling the palms of her hands, transporting her back to more carefree days under the watchful eyes of her cantankerous grandmother.

The warm easterly wind blew across the hills, bending the long stems towards the old metal and wooden farmhouse that sat proudly, like an island, in the middle of the sea of corn. She circled the premises, stalking its layout and calculating her options. The single-floored main house was at the centre of a compound, guarded by two large metal-framed barns. A quick scan of the buildings showed only two human heat sources present in the main building. There were between twenty and thirty other heat sources shared between the barns that resembled cows, although some were considerably larger than the typical livestock.

After her third reconnaissance of the compound, she decided it was safe to move in. Using the field as cover, she made her way round to the front of the main building. She quickly cut across the dusty access road, staying low behind the farming vehicles. She wanted this mission sorted quickly and without a hitch. But, as she started to make her way across the open area towards the front veranda, that all went out of the window.

With a flash of high-powered lights, the whole courtyard was illuminated and there were the sounds of pneumatics as ten feet posts rose from the ground just inside the small wooden fence. They were tall and curved outwards, creating a lipped effect, and in unison immediately began to emanate a distinct high resonating buzz that filled the air with static and the unmistakable taste that only a laser field could generate.

Damn it!

DNA scanners or maybe pressure pads? She had walked straight into them. Ronnie had hoped this world was not as technologically advanced, but that evidently was not the case. She had got sloppy. She was tired and needed rest, but that was not always possible. She was on the move constantly, never sure of her surroundings, never sure of who or what was safe or not. Maybe the fields and farm had made her less cautious. She had allowed herself to be caught up in a nostalgic moment. Lured into a false sense of security. This place reminded her so very much of her grandmother's farm back home. She cursed herself again, *Idiot!*

Okay. Clear your head, she told herself.

Assess the situation.

Gather intel.

Work out possible courses of action.

She paused, took a deep breath to refocus herself and then started to take in as much as she could. The faint hue from the green laser field encircled the building and the barns and, from what she could see, there was no entrance or exit. The release must be inside the main building or, more probably, which would make it more of a problem, on the owner of the property. The seemingly impenetrable barrier was tall and curved outwards to stop any sort of attempts of getting in and, more significantly, it looked just as good at stopping anyone escaping too. The numerous bright spotlights that had powered up shone from above the main building and barns covering the compound, leaving no centimetre of the land unbathed in its searching light. There was no point in retreating or trying to conceal her presence, so instead of meekly seeking some cover, she confidently moved forward, using the tech on her lower arm to scan the building as she did so, ensuring she knew exactly where the two occupants were. As she reached the wooden steps that led up onto the veranda, she stopped instinctively to glance up and down, to make sure there were no hidden surprises. The space was clear except for a pair of differing sized rocking chairs, which looked hand crafted because of the uneven and unsymmetrical nature of their construction.

Reassured, she began to move forward but stopped as the large wooden front doors of the property opened slowly, sliding away into the walls either side of the entrance. Experience forced her to move back, creating a buffer zone between her and the unknown individuals within the silent agrarian residence.

Her wait was short. Stooping slightly to pass through the entrance stepped a bearded giant of a man. He looked to be well over six foot tall, although the long-developed hunch that he stood with disguised his true height. He stood broad shouldered and impassive in expression in front of the entrance, creating a large human shield, dressed in farming fatigues, a well-worn chequered shirt rolled up to the elbows, and huge work boots. He would have been an imposing figure as it was but it was the large weapon that he had shouldered, pointing directly at her, that caught her immediate attention. Damn the infrared scanners. They never picked up weapons. It was unlike any weapon she had ever seen or encountered before, but there was no doubt what it was.

"STOP THERE!" he bellowed loudly but, despite his size and stature, not aggressively. "Do you know you're on private land, young miss?"

"I am sorry," answered Ronnie, holding her hands up slowly so he could see she was unarmed. "I didn't realise."

"Well now you do! You can leave because we aren't in the market to buy anything!"

"I am not selling anything, mister," Ronnie replied calmly.

"Then what's your business here?" growled the man from his raised vantage point, scrunching his large face at her.

"I'm just looking for my mother. I think she may have travelled this way recently," Ronnie replied cautiously, putting her arms behind her back.

"We don't get many visitors in these parts," answered the man. "Whoever told you she came here was mistaken."

"Wasn't so much a person who told me," Ronnie answered, watching the man's face carefully for any glimmer of a reaction. "More a trail she left behind."

"A trail of what?" demanded the man, the weapon rising again a little more tensely.

Ronnie stared up at the man and weighed up her options. She could lie and con her way around this, which would take time, or she could be honest, which carried a risk.

"Particles," she replied.

"A trail of particles?"

"Yes, that's it, I tracked her particles," she repeated honestly.

"You're a tracker, you say? Well, it must be wrong, 'cause there's only me here and my steers," he lied, gesturing towards the barn to the east with the end of the long barrel of the weapon, which he then returned to train back on her. It had been the merest moment of an opening, but Ronnie decided not to react. The distance between them was too much, and his sheer size and higher vantage point gave him the advantage. So, she kept her hands behind her back, although now she gently sorted out some protection of her own from the confines of the pack on her back.

"Okay... well, maybe I could ask them then if they saw her? Her name is Margaret Clemence. She calls herself Maggie."

"Like I said, we haven't seen anyone for quite a while now."

"How about your wife? Maybe she has seen her, spoken to her, helped her. It's really important I find her."

"My wife… she doesn't…" he paused for a moment. "How old are you, kid?"

"I'm fifteen, sir, sixteen in November. Although not quite sure what date we are on here, is it summer?" she asked, not quite sure.

"It's June 24th today…" he began to answer and then stopped as the door behind him opened again and out stepped a woman. It never ceased to amaze her, no matter how many times she first set eyes on her, how it made her heart fill with joy. Seeing her face again, the hair wasn't always the same colour, but it was wild and untameable. She was never dressed in the same manner but she had the unmistakable demeanour of a person who was strong and independent. But the eyes were always the same piercing green and full of life. No matter which version of her she met, those never changed.

Inevitably the joy was short-lived. The hope dashed and the fall in heart followed when she realised it wasn't her. But no matter how many times it happened – it was twenty-seven by her reckoning now – she still had the hope that one day it wouldn't be a look-alike, it wouldn't be this world's version of her. One day it would be her mother. One day she would finally find her.

"Maggie was here," the lady responded, placing her hand on the barrel of the weapon, encouraging her companion to lower it, whilst looking about the compound as if the words she were saying were laced with some sort of destructive power. "You better come inside. She left something for you."

The woman turned and disappeared back into the house,

leaving her companion behind staring down at Ronnie. The weapon he had been brandishing so aggressively was now in one hand, held at its midway point. He took a scuffed step backwards, shrugged his hunched shoulders and then turned, stooping as he too disappeared inside the building. The doors remained invitingly open, tempting Ronnie inside, but she waited for a moment. Experience had taught her not to rush into a situation without taking stock. She had learned that the hard way, and yet something was telling her that this was worth the risk. Quickly scanning the building again, she could see that both individuals had retreated further into its interior, so tentatively she made her way up the steps and into the structure.

From the outside, she had been expecting something more like her grandmother's rural rustic farmhouse, but the inside of the building was somewhat of a surprise. She passed through a short entry hall that then opened out into a large open-plan space, which was lit by a clear transparent roof section above.

The area was metallic, minimalistic and very practical in its design. In fact, it felt more like a laboratory than somewhere you'd reside. If it hadn't have been for the metal-framed sofas and chairs, which looked more accustomed to a doctors' waiting room, she would have said that was what it was. Directly behind the sitting area sat a clinically set out kitchen and eating area, as metallic and sterile as the rest of the room, but it was the wall opposite that caught Ronnie's eye the most. It stood in stark contrast to the rest of the large area, filling the entire wall with shelf upon shelf of books. A moveable ladder leant against the shelves nonchalantly waiting to be called into action. The wall tantalised Ronnie. It had been a long time since she had sat and read. Far too long. But now was not the time.

Around the room, there were five other doors that she presumed led off to bedrooms and bathrooms. It was from one of these that the woman who resembled her mother returned, carrying a metal box. She laid it down on the low metal and glass table, taking a seat on the sofa, and beckoned Ronnie over to sit near her.

"Would you like some tea or a hot beverage?" she asked. "If you're anything like Maggie, you'd maybe like to partake in some tea."

She was right, of course. Her mother did like tea. A clever little snippet to help to lower Ronnie's guard. She'd have to do better than that.

"What's in the box?" enquired Ronnie being deliberately direct.

"Goodness me, you are your mother's daughter, aren't you?" smiled the lady. "Don't you even want to know my name? Or how we came to get to know your mother?"

"I apologise, but as you can imagine I'm keen to find out where my mother is. So, if you have any idea of where she is, I would truly appreciate it if you could tell me," Ronnie urged determinedly.

"Where she is I couldn't tell you. I can tell you what we know of her time with us and some of where she had been, if that is of any help?" offered the woman with a reassuring smile.

"Okay," replied Ronnie, suddenly feeling more than a

little rude. Her mother would not have been impressed. "I'm sorry. What is your name?"

"My name is Freja and this is my custodian Lasse. He is my companion, protector and a helper of sorts." The large man mountain of a man nodded his head solemnly, making Ronnie wonder if he was more a servant.

"Custodian?" she asked.

"Yes. He was assigned to me when I was younger. We all have our companions here. Your mother was surprised too when we discussed it, but we had plenty of time, of which I'm guessing you don't feel we have."

"I don't… why did you have plenty of time with my mother?"

"When Lasse found her, she was injured," answered Freja solemnly.

"Injured how?" asked Ronnie quickly, trying to stifle a worried gasp, which still escaped, giving away her true emotions.

"I can assure you not in a bad way, but enough that she needed rest and time to recover before moving on. It is my understanding that she got into some trouble before she managed the 'jump' from the world she had been on."

"Some trouble? With whom?"

"The authorities on that world, but she managed to escape them and 'jump' here to this world."

"So she explained she 'jumped'?" said Ronnie, relieved that her mother had been able to trust this likeness, this lady enough to share her secrets.

"Travelling from world to world. Yes, we had time. We discussed many things once she trusted me. About her journey, about you and your grandfather, about her work. I also shared some of my own knowledge and work with her. It was a well spent time for both of us."

"So when she left she was okay?"

"Yes. When she jumped, which I must say was an impressive sight, she was fully recovered. Please come and sit with me," urged Freja, tapping the space next to her on the sofa.

"She didn't say where she was going?" Ronnie answered, refusing to move from her standing position. She may have been feeling more relaxed, but she still wanted the reassurance of knowing she was closest to the exit.

"No, although it is my understanding that the jumps are random in their nature, she hadn't worked out a way of controlling them, which is one of the answers she was seeking."

Ronnie breathed a sigh of relief. It was good to hear her mother was safe and well or had been the last time she had been seen. This knowledge filled her with renewed hope and belief.

"When did she leave?" asked Ronnie, determined to gather as much intel as possible.

"Around two weeks ago," Freja answered, motioning to Lasse, who moved back into the kitchen and began to collect together items from cupboards.

"Then I am getting closer," sighed Ronnie.

"How far were you behind?"

"When I first started searching for her it was just shy of six months, but each jump I am getting closer. I don't spend as much time on the worlds she has jumped to, I think maybe because she has to work out the world, but when I get there, I am just following her particle trail."

"Yes, how do you manage that?"

"Honestly... I am not quite sure. My grandfather is a Quantum Physicist and he created a device for me to track and follow my mother's particles. Apparently, he says we all have a unique particle trail that can be tracked if you have the right technology."

"Your mother told me all about your Quantum Physics and what she had been trying to do. I profess to not understand everything she spoke about but it was truly fascinating."

"Yes she is one too. A very talented and creative mind..." Ronnie paused as Lasse returned and placed a large platter of food in front of them; breads, meats and cheeses. Suddenly she realised how hungry she was.

"Come and sit," pleaded Freja. "Come and eat. You must be hungry from your journey."

"Yes, I am," admitted Ronnie, moving towards the table, her rumbling stomach urging her forward. Cautiously she sat down, making sure Freja and Lasse were both still in her line of sight. She gingerly took a piece of bread from the platter, and it was warm. Fresh oven-baked bread. Her mouth instantly began to water in anticipation of biting into it. But as she lifted it to her mouth, she stopped, her newly acquired instinct of self-preservation kicking in.

"I assure you there is nothing wrong with the food, look..." And with that, Freja picked up some bread, meat and cheese and made a small sandwich before taking a large bite from it. "It's delicious," she remarked with a smirk and her mouth full.

It was all the encouragement that Ronnie needed, throwing caution to the wind she tucked into the platter, making numerous small sandwiches, and then eagerly feasting on them. Feeding the space in her stomach that she had been ignoring for too long.

"So, what's in the box?" asked Ronnie between bites, returning her attention back to the grey, metal object on the table.

"Ah yes, this is a box that your mother left for you," Freja answered matter of factly.

"WHAT?" spluttered Ronnie.

"Maggie said that if anyone followed her it would be you, but she also said there might be others, who might be more aggressive in trying to find her. Hence Lasse and the blaster."

"She knows I am looking for her," said Ronnie, more a statement than a question.

"Yes, but I think it was more of a feeling, a hope, than her actually knowing. Although it would appear she was correct to assume so."

"So, what's in it?" Ronnie asked again, reaching down and picking it up, passing it from one hand to the other, weighing it up.

"I have no idea," answered Freja.

"You haven't looked inside it? You're not curious?" Ronnie asked with disbelief.

"Oh, I am most curious. But your mother said it was for you and so attempting to look inside would mean breaking my promise to her. Besides—" added Freja with a knowing smile— "only you can open it. She DNA coded the lock so that only you could access it."

"How did she have my DNA?"

"A lock of your hair in a locket," answered Freja, motioning around her neck as she spoke. "A beautiful locket."

Ronnie fell silent. She knew which locket she meant. It had been her grandmother's and a family heirloom. She had never realised it had had her hair inside it.

She turned the box over in her hand and found the pad that she needed. As she placed her thumb onto it, a small tingling sensation spread across the skin and then, with a small hiss, the box opened. She slid it open to find a metal arm bracelet, not unlike the one she already wore on her right lower forearm. It was similar in design but looked like her mother had made some alterations to the original design spec.

Suddenly, the interior of the room lit up an ambient orange, and a holograph of the surrounding area appeared above the table. Freja rose to her feet and studied it carefully. There were twenty or so red dots making their way through the fields towards the building.

"Lasse," she said, turning calmly to her custodian. "We have more guests and these are unwanted ones, take Ronnie out to the fields, and then come back, she must make haste and jump. Show her where her mother left from and then return here so we can make our guests feel welcome."

★★★

Jamie Lewis is a 46-year-old writer, teacher and father (rearrange dependent on time of day or particular crisis at hand) who has been scribbling, typing and telling stories for a number of years now, whether that be in class or on paper. His desire to write firstly came from years of telling stories to his own children and classes of children, having fun creating versions of stories in different genres attached to the curriculum and for different ages. More recently (the last two or three years) writing has given him the opportunity to explore the urge to develop his own ideas, giving them faces, voices and freedom to tell their own stories, in short story and longer novel forms.

AN UNWILLINGNESS TO GIVE UP

Gemma Spurling

"An unwillingness to give up, despite everyone advising her otherwise" had been the way CJ's university mentor had described her. Her unfailing urge to prove herself and show the world what she could be had been her defining characteristic from as early as she could remember. Yet now in the almost complete darkness of her room at 2.17am, she felt it was finally time to admit defeat. She lay nearly paralysed with pain; cocooned in her duvet and unable to sleep. A cold sweat clung to her spine as her mind raced trying to identify just exactly where her life had gone wrong. Her whole left side tingled as if fire ants were crawling beneath her skin. Pain shot down from her temple into her eye and jaw. She felt trapped. Completely and utterly trapped in a broken body when her soul yearned for more.

Life had never been easy for Charlotte Julie Porter. Named after her mother's favourite Bronte and her father's favourite aunt, CJ had always been smart, ambitious, and quite frankly a bit of a show-off. She'd alienated herself from her peers at a young age by being a bit too much of a teacher's pet and not particularly girlie. Preferring the company of boys, but not exactly a tomboy and no good at football either, she'd felt adrift in a world where other children seemed to know who to be friends with and just how to do it. As she'd grown up, her eagerness to fit in and her ever-growing fear of failure made her try way too hard when she did make friends.

In her early teen years this had led to many embarrassing and foolish mistakes trying to fit in. The worst of these was the time CJ had attempted shoplifting in Claire's Accessories on a dare, whilst trying to impress a group of schoolfriends. Having surreptitiously dropped several pairs of earrings into her bag, she'd walked out of the shop towards where the girls were waiting, feeling like she might finally be accepted as one of the cool girls, when suddenly she'd felt a hand grab her left shoulder. Seeing the girls run away as fast as their legs could carry them as she was turned back around into the shop had been one of the most humiliating moments of her life.

The same old patterns repeated themselves as CJ moved through life. She continually tried too hard, with friendships, with school and university work, and with jobs, and she ended up the one hurt at the end. CJ always 'burnt the candle at both ends', as her grandmother used to say, fearing that if she wasn't putting her all in then she wouldn't be good enough, and ended up burning out. She'd worked so hard that she had made herself ill before her A-level exams, in her final year of university and during her teacher training, meaning she'd never really achieved the results she had wanted for herself or been told she was capable of.

The years of trying her best and always falling before the final hurdle was what led to her being in this state at 2.17am in her darkened bedroom with the clock beside her bed ticking ever so slowly on.

CJ had been lying there watching her clock for three hours and forty-two minutes now. Her heartbeat was pulsing through her body so loudly it was making her head pound. She could feel it like waves, moving from her stomach up to her ears and back down again. Her body ached as though she had run a marathon, with the flu, the previous day. In reality, she had simply laid on the sofa watching old episodes of *Friends* on Netflix while trying to keep herself from crying in front of her kids, trying to remember what day of the week it was.

For the past fourteen months that had been CJ's life, she'd waded through treacle on a daily basis, with the odd glimmer of joy from her son's first rugby match, her daughter's first day of school and her husband's promotion. But the days had blurred into a never-ending quagmire of emptiness. She felt trapped. Completely and utterly trapped. A classic over achiever, wanting to be perfect at everything she did, she had worked herself so hard in the first twenty-seven years of her life that she began to break.

This woman who was so driven and high achieving by nature was now trapped in a body that refused to do even the simplest tasks. To shower took gargantuan effort. Had her children not needed to eat she wouldn't have even opened the fridge most days. The house was either a total bombsite or looked as though fairies had been and cleaned it in the night when her husband and children were sleeping, because CJ could not. The days after these sleepless nights were the ones when CJ posted photos of her children playing in their lovely tidy home on Facebook with a cutesy caption about how much fun it was being at home with them. Sometimes she even took photos to share on a different day – the Herculean task of hiding how much she was failing from the world.

"That's not what Astrid was wearing today, is it?" her husband had said on one such evening last week.

"She was dressed this morning, but she got some paint on it. I changed her into her PJs by the time you came home from work," CJ lied. She couldn't let him know what a terrible mother she was for letting the kids stay in their pyjamas all day during the school holidays, she'd thought to herself.

"Oh, fair enough," he'd replied, looking back at his phone. "Did you see the post Phil shared earlier? The meme about last night's footy? It was so funny!"

CJ gave only a vague sound as a reply, but he hadn't seemed to notice. It was scary how easy it was to hide how she was feeling, even from her husband.

The clock had finally ticked over to 2.18am by the time CJ had run all this through in her mind and she let out a sorrowful sigh. *Is this my life now?* she thought. *Am I ever going to feel normal again? Or is this my normal now?* The pain coursing through CJ's body had no real cause that she could identify. She hadn't hurt herself, hadn't fallen or been in an accident. It had just appeared one day, like an unwelcome salesperson knocking at the door and barging their way in to your house. With there being no discernible cause, CJ could not fathom a way to 'fix' herself, nor had she seemed able to muster any impetus to try over the past year. It was impossible. There was no way it was going to change or get better. CJ knew, as clearly as she knew that the sky was blue, that there was just no fixing her. She was broken. She would be broken forever.

The message running over and over in her mind told CJ that if she was broken forever then she was just a huge burden to her family. She had nothing to offer her husband or children. Her friends, the ones she had worked so hard to get, wouldn't want anything to do with her if she couldn't do things for them. Why would they? What was the point in her being here? Wouldn't they all be better off if she weren't here? Sure, it would be tough for her husband at first, but he would find someone new. Someone who could be a better wife to him, a better mother to their children, someone who wouldn't drag him down.

It wasn't the first time these thoughts had haunted CJ in the early hours of the morning as she lay in the dark. But she decided it would be the last. She couldn't bear being in this amount of pain for another day, another sleepless night, even another hour.

CJ slipped out of bed and crept to the bathroom, careful not to wake her husband. In the harsh light of the bathroom mirror, CJ examined her face. At just twenty-nine, her skin looked grey and old. She pulled her face this way and that as she examined the bags under her eyes, big enough to carry a week's worth of shopping for a family of eight, and realised that her eyes themselves had lost all of the sparkle her husband had always said that he loved. Her smile, once her favourite of her features, seemed to have lost its ability to spread across her face or reach her eyes, and her teeth now remained hidden when she tried to force herself to smile.

Leaving the bathroom, she tiptoed into Astrid's room. Her darling daughter's hair was smeared across her face in a sweaty tangle and her body contorted in a position that CJ could not fathom how it was comfortable. CJ moved over to Astrid's bed and kissed her gently on her forehead, terrified to wake her but needing to kiss her before she left. Astrid's hot sticky breath clung to CJ's tear-streaked cheeks as she lay her head for a moment on the pillow.

"Goodbye my sweet girl," CJ said in a barely audible whisper, "look after Daddy and Daniel for me."

CJ paused for a moment in the hallway and let an echoing sob escape her. Could she really do this? Did she have a choice? As pain ricocheted around her body and made her feel barely able to stand, she knew that she did not.

She then stole into Daniel's room. He could be such a handful but her miracle boy, the one her doctors had said she would never conceive but who had given her eight years as a mother, looked like a perfect angel when he slept. Again, she kissed her child on the forehead and her heart swelled with love and pain. Would her children spend the rest of their lives hating her for this act of selfishness? Whispering a goodbye, she hoped they would understand and find it in their hearts to forgive her.

Padding cautiously down the stairs, avoiding the two halfway down that squeaked like very chatty mice and running her fingers across the spot on the wallpaper where Astrid had drawn what she'd said was a cat but looked more like a spiky blob with a thin wiggly tail in Sharpie, CJ made her way to the kitchen. She sat shivering at the kitchen table with a pen in her hand and a sheet of paper. Her fingers ached as she struggled to hold the pen steady, her hands contorted like a ninety-year-old's. She quickly wrote a simple set of instructions to her husband and folded the paper, placing it in front of the kettle.

Locating her wellies, keys and coat, she silently opened the front door and stepped outside into the street. Her thick, navy coat over the top of her pyjamas was surprisingly warm on the cold autumnal morning and, locking the door behind her, CJ set off along the road towards the centre of her village. Passing the village school, CJ felt another wave of heartbreak as the clouds parted and the full moon shone brightly onto her daughter's classroom door. *Please*, she thought, *please let them forgive me and be happy.*

Checking her watch, she picked up her speed. It was somehow nearly 4am already, the time since she had made her decision and climbed out of bed seemed to have slipped by her in the blink of an eye. CJ didn't want to be meeting the early dog walkers as she reached the reservoir; being found too soon and her pain continuing was something she could not risk. She walked along the path where the dappled trees blocked the bright moonlight to the far end of the reservoir, a place she had so frequently brought her children to sit on the bench, feed the ducks and look for frogs. Her breath caught in her throat as CJ rounded the corner to her final destination. Here the darkness of the trees gave way to a silvery pool of light. Moonlight played on the surface as the water was rippled by the breeze.

"Such a beautiful place," CJ sighed to herself. It was almost enough to make her doubt what she had come here to do.

Almost.

CJ stood with her eyes closed in the moonlight for a moment, feeling the pain course through her achy body like electricity and yet she felt so at peace. Discarding her coat on the bench, she walked to the water's edge.

*

At 6.03am, five-year-old Astrid appeared sleepy eyed and messy haired in her parents' bedroom. She looked at the bed, but something wasn't right. Her little face scrunched up in confusion. She padded wearily across the landing to the bathroom, rubbing her left eye whilst clutching her boo-bear comforter in her right hand. Her face scrunched even more.

She headed back to her parents' room and poked her father's cheek with a pudgy finger, causing him to stir and groggily open one eye.

"Where's Mummy?" she asked.

"What's up, kiddo?" He yawned, stretching an arm up into the air.

"Where's Mummy?"

"Is she in the toilet?"

"No Daddy, I went and see-ed in there!"

"She's probably downstairs, my angel." He pulled himself up and sat blinking for a moment. Astrid just stared at him impatiently. "Shall we go and find her?" he asked.

They headed down the stairs, missing the two in the middle that squeaked like chatty mice and running their fingers over Astrid's Sharpie artwork. In the kitchen, Astrid looked around the kitchen and, realising her mother wasn't there, then ran off to check the living room. Michael spotted CJ's note with his name on leaning against the kettle and wandered over to it. He unfolded the paper and read the words his wife had left him:

"Police. The bench at the far end of the reservoir. DO NOT COME. Stay with the children. I love you but I can't fight this battle with myself every day anymore. Tell Astrid and Daniel I love them, every single day of their lives. I'm sorry."

★★★

This is Gemma's first foray into writing. She has always wanted to become a published author so this is a dream come true. Gemma lives in Leicestershirre with her husband, son and cat. She is an independent travel agent working from home so that she can spend as much time as possible with her amazing eight-year-old son. She says, "I want my story to show people the depths that depression can take somebody to and help raise awareness and understanding for this awful condition, having suffered with it myself on and off for many years."

You can find out more about Gemma Here:
https://www.instagram.com/gemma_spurling_travelforjoy/

THE CROSSED KEYS GHOST

Laura Goodsell

The streets are filled with animal waste. Rotting vegetables, thick sticky mud and smells you would never wish on your worst enemy. Yet here I am, unable to see or hear any of it, my mind on just one thing. My heart pounding, head rushing, my mouth dry. I look down at my sweaty hot palms. Stumbling, I sway to the left, then right myself, tears stinging my sore eyes. Seeing an empty lane to the side, I veer in, I need to get away from here. Oh, what have I done?

Twenty-four hours earlier

The year is 1720 and in a small village just a few hours' walk from the city of Hunting, lived William and Elizabeth. William was a cobbler by trade, his small business originally belonging to his father. He took it over after his passing last year. William and his father never really had a great relationship, so no love lost. Tradition dictated that he follow in his footsteps, so to speak.

Walking along the hot, dusty highroad into the city, others passing by on their horses, William and Elizabeth's only horse was needed on their small holding, which Elizabeth ran. He began to think about his life, again. A country boy at heart, he really didn't want to be in the hustle and bustle of this busy life; too many people, too many worries and too many crimes. Not to mention the constant fear of disease and illness. He was happier working on the land, or elsewhere. Selling the business had been on his mind lately, but the money was badly needed.

Arriving at the cobblers, William got to work. His mind really wasn't on the day, it never was, because you see William had a secret, a BIG secret. He had met someone a few months back, someone who had become an integral part of his life. It all started out casual, then the odd drink led to secret alleyway meets. The more they met, the more serious it became, meeting in secret at the Crossed Keys Public House at the top of the hill.

They were both planning on meeting that night, meaning William was making more than a few mistakes at work. He couldn't concentrate, he was excited, however very aware they had been careless, reckless. The growing love had made them forgetful and take silly risks. Unfortunately, it was not just the fact William was married, that was bad enough, but there were other reasons.

Their love could get them killed.

As evening drew near, William locked up and made his

way up the hill towards the Crossed Keys Pub nervous, excited, worried and fearful, too many emotions, but it was all worth it.

Meanwhile, two streets over, Elizabeth held her hand up to shield her eyes from the dying sun. She was meant to be at her sister's farmhouse, but it had to be done. This was it, this was the last time she would be embarrassed. Ducking down alleys and side streets, taking the longer route to avoid passing her husband's cobblers, Elizabeth soon found herself face to face with the Crossed Keys Public House.

She had known about the affair for a while, tried to forget it, tried to ignore it, but the hurt and anger she felt had begun to overwhelm her; it niggled at her very core. She couldn't go on like this, otherwise she would end up in the asylum. It had to end today.

Elizabeth hoisted up her skirts to avoid the slop that was called a street and marched on. A hot flush engulfed her body as she stepped over the threshold. There were regulars at the few tables, a few of the old boys eyeing her, wondering what a woman was doing there, but they didn't really care. Elizabeth stopped and looked around, saw the entrance to the bed chambers, knowing this was where her husband was conducting his affair. She just wasn't sure which room. Luckily, the Crossed Keys only had three in total. It was a small public house rather than an inn.

Silently walking up the stairs to the rooms, Elizabeth's emotions outweighed any sense she may have had; what she was about to do had to be done. She couldn't go on like this. "It has to be done," was her mantra these days.

Pushing on the first door it swung open, showing an empty room. She continued down the hall to the second door. Elizabeth took a deep breath and pushed. It swung open silently. She froze. There he was, in the semi dark, standing in the window. Looking out, he hadn't heard her come in. She couldn't make out any features, her eyes were watery, her vision blurred, but the hatred had taken over. Elizabeth pulled a small blade out from between her skirts and ran directly at him.

Hitting him square in the back, the force pushed him forwards. Stumbling, he swung round to face his attacker. Elizabeth recoiled back, hands to her face. No, it couldn't be. He fell backwards, hitting a chair as he went down, crumpling on the floor at an odd angle.

Dead.

Elizabeth opened her mouth to scream but nothing escaped. Heart pounding, she fell forwards, violently sick near the bed. Shaking, with sweat dripping, the "what have I done?" panic set in. Elizabeth turned and ran, straight down the corridor, past curious onlookers, out into the busy street. People were looking at her, curious eyes and disapproving looks, and she stumbled. Her head was spinning. She had to get away from here, as far away as possible. What had she done?

Three hundred years later on 12th June 2020, Graham Winters and his team of paranormal experts were preparing their equipment for what they hoped would be an eventful night.

It had been another sweltering day. As evening drew near, Graham welcomed the breeze it brought. He had to admit, as he sat outside having a cigarette, that he was quite skeptical of this particular investigation. He had heard so many stories of a ghost haunting the Crossed Keys Pub, they were all different apart from one fact; their ghost didn't seem to like women. Many female visitors had experienced being pushed or shoved. At fifty-eight, he was not so young anymore, and was hoping they would all be safe throughout the investigation. He felt it was a big ask for anything to really happen. However, they had been hired to do a job. A local TV station was interested in making the Crossed Keys Pub haunting into a documentary.

Walking back into reception, he bumped into his lead cameraman. 'Hey, James, how's everything? Are you all set up?' he asked.

'Yeah, pretty much now, it's a bit awkward, isn't it?' James answered.

'What is?'

'Well, you know, the Crossed Keys ghost.'

Graham chuckled at this.

James looked around him. 'With so many sightings, how do we know which area to start in?' He felt uncomfortable being here.

'You'll be fine. I know what you mean, though. I think room two is right, majority of the sightings have happened in that area. Don't worry, it will be okay, nothing may happen at all.' Graham turned to leave.

'Yeah, you're right. Anyway, I'm heading down to the bar. Care to join me for a nightcap?'

'Sure, why not, may help with your nerves!' They both laughed.

At midnight, the whole team were assembled in room two. It was a reasonable sized room, fitting several people comfortably. As well as Graham and James, they also had Sheila the producer/presenter for the TV show, and her makeup artist Kate sitting on the bed – she was local to the area and had always been fascinated with the occult – a second cameraman Dave, and finally Tim and Rob, brothers who had made the paranormal their lives, all made up the team. What they didn't know about ghosts wasn't worth knowing. They also had an in-depth knowledge of all the equipment used at investigations.

James counted down with his fingers, three, two, one, and Sheila stood tall with her hair piled high and perfect makeup and introduced the show. 'Hello and welcome to a special one-off documentary on the ghost of the Crossed Keys Pub in Hunting, where it is supposedly haunted by a ghost that has got physical during encounters. We believe the ghost to be female and many women have reported incidences of being pushed, shoved or physically moved. We're here tonight on 12th June to discover if she really exists and if the hundreds of sightings over the years are credible.'

Sheila then introduced the team to the viewers.

After sitting about for an hour and a half, with James still filming, Sheila wondered if they would get anything newsworthy. Just as she got up and raised her arms to stretch, she felt a cold breeze sweep over her. It chilled her to the very bone. Graham, who was sitting near her on the bed, shivered and everyone exchanged knowing glances; they weren't alone.

'Is there anyone there?' Sheila called. 'Anyone at all?' All but the two cameramen stood and held hands in a circle. Sheila called out again and then Tim jumped in shock; something had touched him and he broke the circle.

A cold chill had descended over them. They were breathing out steam, all looking round, on edge, terrified, when James let go of his camera. It hit the floor with a sickening thud, and the others spun round at the crash.

'James, are you okay?' Graham was worried.

'Yeah, I'm fine, I just got spooked is all. Damn, my camera!' He bent down to check out the damage.

'We need to approach this in another way, we need to call on them through the Ouija board. Let's really find out who we have here,' Graham announced.

While the board was being set out, Kate was in the back doing some of her own research. There had been many stories about this hotel over the years, and something was niggling at the back of her mind, there was something familiar about this place. Scrolling through different news articles on her phone, she came across some very interesting history on the Crossed Keys Pub. Back before the building had become a pub, a young lad had been caught stealing a loaf of bread. With the local jails full, people were kept in local houses until the courts were open. The lad had been kept in the cellar of the building and tried to start a fire to weaken the latch but it was too strong, the fire took hold and the boy died; could this be him? Another article dating back to 1720 referenced the murder of a gentleman in the hotel, the body found in an upstairs room, knife sticking out of his back, no signs of a struggle or killer, no one ever prosecuted. Their ghost was presumed female, could there be a link somewhere with these old tales?

The board was set, the lights dimmed, more for the camera than actually helpful, but it had the desired effect, everyone went silent. The air was thick with anticipation, all were on edge.

Sheila spoke first, startling a few crew members. 'We're all gathered here to find out the name and circumstance surrounding the haunting of the Crossed Keys Pub.' She closed her eyes, and touched the glass, the others following suit, Kate, Graham, Dave and Rob all leaning forward.

'Is someone here?' Sheila spoke softly, almost a whisper. 'Is someone here?' she repeated. Waiting.

Nothing happened. Just as Sheila was about to ask again, Kate flew backwards, shrieking, 'Something hit me!' shaking all over. Sheila glared at her, willing her to stop acting so daft in front of the cameras. Composing herself under Sheila's glare, they all reached for the glass again.

This time Sheila asked, 'What is your name?' The glass jittered, nearly falling, but slowly moved around the board, spelling W I L L.

'Will? Is that your name? Or is that who killed you?' Sheila looked quizzically at Kate, they thought this spirit was a woman; wasn't it?

Silence.

Cutting for a break, Sheila and Kate made their way to the van to make themselves a stiff coffee, while the boys got out of there for some fresh air.

'That was strange. Who is Will? I'd love to find out who they really are and why they are here. But with just the word Will, we can't even do that. Who are they looking for? So many unanswered questions.' Sheila sat down with a thump.

'Well…' Kate ventured. 'There is this story of a murder here around 1700, maybe a little later, a man was killed. It was said to have been a revenge murder, but nothing was ever really written about it. I couldn't find his name, but I may have found a woman by the name of Elizabeth who could have been involved. I found out she later ended up in an asylum. No one ever claimed to know her, she appeared to have been disowned. As though she'd embarrassed or humiliated her family, you know what life was like back then. Maybe this could be her?'

'Maybe. Certainly sounds interesting. Maybe this is the spirit that's been haunting this place for 300 years? Maybe not. Let's try asking. What do you know about this murder?' Sheila sipped her coffee.

'Not a lot. A gentleman-class man was murdered in 1719-21, dates are sketchy. Reports state another man was involved but never found. A woman left the scene in a state, but after extensive searches they never found her. It was just with my research that I put Elizabeth possibly at the scene of this murder.'

'You think this could be the woman Elizabeth? Come back, looking for…? I'm not sure, the missing man perhaps? Let's try it, if anything it will be good for ratings to get at least a little story behind this.' Sheila drained her mug.

Heading back in, they all gathered around the board, fingers poised, feeling a little more composed in front of the cameras now they had a plan.

Sheila spoke. 'Can you tell us the year please?' The glass pointed to the numbers 1720.

After several more safe questions, Sheila ventured, 'Miss Elizabeth, please can you tell us how you died?'

The glass was yanked out of their hands and thrown violently at the wall, smashing.

They all looked at each other, eyes wide; what on earth was going on?

Sheila stood and stretched her back. They'd decided to cut there, as it was beginning to get a little out of hand; no-one was having fun anymore, this was actually quite scary, the tension was thick.

'Right, we need to finish this. On or off air I wanna get out of here soon.' Graham was getting concerned for his crew. 'Let's work this together. The Ouija board didn't give us much, but things we do know are: there is definitely a spirit here, the name Will, 1720 and a story from around this time that Kate dug up of a murder and a possible asylum victim. So, who do we think this is?'

'Honestly, I wonder if it's a she at all? Look at the anger with which the glass flew,' Kate suggested.

'But that was because I asked how she'd died,' Sheila said.

'No, I think it was because you said "she". What if this is a man?'

'Interesting thought,' Graham mused, 'let's give it one more go.'

Standing in a circle one last time, everyone was holding hands. Silenced, Sheila asked, 'Is anyone here?' A sudden knock behind them made a few hearts beat faster but no one dared move.

'What is your name?' A low whisper was heard like a gentle breeze sweeping through, but with no movement.

Sheila asked again, 'What is your name? Please make it known.' The whisper was louder this time.

Graham spoke softly, 'Did anyone hear the word William?' A few nodded. *Yes!* he thought, *this is progress.* He nodded to Sheila to continue.

This wasn't the woman they thought it was. This strange spirit that had been shoving women for 300 years, could in fact be a man! What a revelation.

Sheila decided to get to the point. 'Please tell us, why are you here?' Suddenly, Dave broke the circle, stumbled backward, head down, grunting and shaking; where did this come from?

James ventured forward. 'Are you okay?' Sheila stopped him, arm out, shaking her head.

Dave made a low growling sound, quite guttural, and in a low voice he said, 'She knows. She knows,' he repeated. Starting to shake, Sheila could see he was getting upset, she had to get him back on track.

'Can you please tell us why you are here?'

'Meeting someone, where is he?'

'Who?' said Sheila. 'Who are you meeting?'

'Charles, where is Charles?' Dave growled.

'Charles isn't here, is Charles a friend?' Sheila looked around. 'Can you tell us who Charles is? We are here to help.'

A long silence, then: 'He's my lover.'

A few gasps from around the room but everyone was frozen, not daring to move, they wanted to know the rest now they had the spirit's attention.

'Who knows about you and Charles, Will?'

'My wife, she knows.'

'Who is your wife?' asked Sheila, not wanting to anger him with too many questions, but they needed to know, thinking she may already know, but she had to ask.

'Elizabeth. She found out, she found out,' he said.

'Did Elizabeth kill you?' It was a brave question and from tonight's experience could have provoked an extreme reaction, but Dave just nodded. The sadness in his eyes told it all.

Suddenly, Dave collapsed with sheer exhaustion, covered in sweat. 'What the hell happened?' He looked around at everyone's shocked faces.

'Well, we found out who our ghost is,' Graham told him.

The following morning, the team sat together in the studio's conference room. None of them looked like they had slept in days.

'Last night was amazing,' said Kate.

'I agree,' offered Sheila. 'One of the most amazing, but emotionally draining paranormal experiences I've had.'

As Graham came in, he said, 'Right, Let's piece this together.'

Sitting down, he pulled out his notes from the previous night. 'To sum up, we have a gay ghost called William, who was having an affair with Charles. His wife Elizabeth found out and killed him in the Crossed Keys Pub.'

'I don't believe Elizabeth meant to kill her husband, though,' said Kate. 'I believe she thought it was his lover, remember that article I found? About a woman who ended up in an asylum? Coupled with the woman at the scene seen running away, I think it really was Elizabeth from the asylum and she thought she was stabbing her husband's lover. The shock, grief and guilt took over, she couldn't accept what she had done. I guess not having anyone to talk to slowly drove her mad, so to speak.

'I think you're right, what a sad story,' Graham said.

Looking around the room, everyone sat in silence as though in remembrance of those lost to this tragic tale of sorrow and heartbreak.

★★★

Laura Goodsell lives in Leicestershire with her partner and their two children, enjoying the quiet village lifestyle. She is an award-winning Digital Designer, creating and hosting websites, designing social media graphics and ebooks. During lockdown Laura created and launched the Business Design Academy and she is also a Canva Creator, designing the templates available to the public within Canva. Laura loves to read and has a passion for collecting antique books.

You can find out more about Laura here:
www.anchoronline.co.uk

SOCIAL STANDING

Eve Wallace

The early morning mist swirled like a cyclone around her as she rose from her broken sleep. Bella couldn't remember a night in the last eight months that she had slept through, whilst she lay there, the mist around her; she watched her breath seep out of her mouth and meet the reality of another cold morning. She closed her eyes slowly, breathed deeply and remembered a life that seemed so long ago she was fearful that she may wake one day and not even be able to remember it at all.

The summer had been so long and warm, lazy days at home with nothing to do but socialise and keep up with the in crowd, tennis lessons on a Tuesday, the horses to tend to on a daily basis, brunch on Wednesday and always time in the week for a well-earned manicure or treatment, but there was a constant underlying ache in her, a dull relentless ache Bella hadn't felt since, well, now she had the time and space to think about it, since she had been a small girl; even then she had felt that she never quite fitted in anywhere, not in school or within the social circle she had been born into. Bella knew she was socially awkward but had learned to live with that, finding coping mechanisms to help her look like the well turned out fashionista she had been groomed to be. But, deep down, she hated the attention and large crowds, preferring the company of a few friends, as opposed to some people who loved to be the centre of everyone else's world whether they wanted them to be or not. She was also fully aware that her looks, which had now faded slightly due to circumstances, would have got her far in life, opened doors for her in the fashion or modelling world and found her the husband of everyone's dream. In her old life, yes, but in this life it was dangerous, she had to ensure that she did not draw attention to herself. Her hair, once perfectly tamed and styled, now looked how her whole life felt to her, bedraggled and unkempt. Her beautifully manicured hands, so used to the regularity of file, polish and a hand massage, now grubby and with sore, broken skin where the cold had touched them through the unruly winter just passing.

Life had felt quite carefree in those years before. No money worries with credit cards and a monthly allowance from Daddy, which was increased on each birthday but never discussed with her mother. At the time the money had made up for– and yes, she did admit to herself slightly took the sting out of – those painful years at boarding school, away from the ones you thought you loved for so long. And they chose to send her there. Well, her mother had made the choice, but she could see in her father's tired eyes that there was no use in trying to fight about it; Mother knew best in all situations and that was the end of it, no discussion, just a cold look that spoke a thousand words. So away she went to better her future, a life that had already been mapped out for her. School days at boarding school were bearable, and as she took a deep intake of breath, she could recall the smell of the inside of the dormitories, an ancient mix of oak timber panels and a dampness that lived in the very being of the bricks and mortar itself. In the evening, the heady scent of girls' perfume filled the air; even with nowhere in particular to go, the girls always had to make the upmost effort with their appearance. Supper was always an interesting event, although she felt like she was going through the motions, like a doll being dressed up. But it was without a doubt a pageant-like event every evening; who was wearing what and whose parents had rushed to have delivered the latest must have items to ensure that it wasn't their daughter who would be ridiculed during the evening. Then the pings of phones after supper, selfies here and there being posted on all manner of social medial platforms; who was the most popular?

Lessons were engaging, her teachers the most knowledgeable scholars money could buy and she tried her very best because – contrary to her mother's thoughts that she would marry into money and carry on the family bloodline – she wanted success and to be loved. She was a thoughtful, kind young lady, but she had a point to prove. Mother did not always know best; times had changed and, unfortunately, her mother still lived in the age where marriage and procreation were all women were good for.

Her thoughts returned to school life. Once lessons and

homework had finished and supper had been eaten, that is when it started. The other girls had quickly picked up on her social awkwardness and used it to their advantage to break her at any cost. The taunting of not being clever enough, not being thin enough or pretty enough, not having enough followers had created those tiny fracture lines in her confidence that would only get greater as she got older.

Bella returned from boarding school and to everyone around her she was as expected, a well-rounded young lady. And, surprisingly, to her mother at least, good grades in most subjects. She settled back into life at home and was surrounded with all the latest must haves every girl would dream of, again thanks to Daddy, along with a kiss on the head occasionally to show he cared. And he did care, he loved her so much, his only daughter, the light of his life and the one true beautiful thing he had in his shallow existence, his baby Arabella. But to show affection was a sign of weakness, so an uncomfortable, almost unfamiliar hug or brief kiss was all there was on offer, though she gratefully took every opportunity of affection that her father bestowed on her.

Her mother, Claudette, was a hard creature with features to match; a strong straight nose, arched eyebrows almost permanently giving the impression she was looking down on you, stunning brown hair and a Parisian chic that was just so natural. Immaculate was the word that sprung into Bella's head when she thought of her mother, immaculate and crisp. She was immediately saddened that the initial words springing to mind were not kind, loving, nurturing, fun or caring, but no, immaculate and crisp it was, and always in the right attire for any occasion. Bella giggled to herself when she thought about her mother's nightgown even being crease free. Raised in significant wealth, Claudette's upbringing had been tough, and she saw no sign of yielding where her own daughter was concerned. Why change what she felt had worked well for generations before her? She ruled the house with an iron fist and everyone was terrified of her, including all the house staff, and that was just the way she liked it, keeping everyone in their place, the slight smirk when she was chastising someone giving that away.

Claudette too had attended the same boarding school. It was a family tradition that was not to be broken. She was a most accomplished woman in all the social etiquette and well respected in the right social circles, no time at all for lower classes and definitely not an ounce of empathy running through her bones.

She met her husband Taylor at a polo event. The match had been discussed for many months prior to their meeting by both families, it was agreed that they were of the right social standing and wealth for each other and the rest, as they say, is history. I am sure she grew to love him over the forty-two years of marriage in her own hardened way. She wondered if back in the days when they first met and they were care free, did they have fun and love and enjoy every aspect of each other? Are there old photographs put away somewhere of them laughing together and loving the life they had and the life that was yet to come? Or did the enormity of the wealth and the children weigh heavy on them both with the laughter lessening over time until they just existed and stopped living?

She had two children. A son, Hugo, the first born and heir to the family wealth who was the apple of her eye; the boy could do no wrong on any level. As he got older, his misdemeanours were constantly overlooked, brushed under the carpet or taken care of; the string of unsuitable girlfriends, the social drug taking phase, being fired from numerous jobs. But that didn't matter to him. Jobs were just a way of meeting more of the fairer sex, more fun and frolics to be had. My God, he didn't need the money in any way, the family wealth was extraordinary and would mean that he would never have to do a day's work in his life, but he liked to "play" at being a normal working-class run-of-the-mill chap… that's how he got his kicks. He felt quite insignificant at that moment and her thoughts returned to her mother, the cold dragon. Bella squeezed her eyes tight shut and tried hard to remember a time when the woman had ever shown her any affection, even the slightest glimpse of approval, but nothing came to mind. She assumed that this was part of her memory that had started to slip away over the past eight months. There must have been times when the woman had at least kissed her? But no, all thoughts only led to a strong but bony hand squeezing her shoulder at her beloved grandmother's funeral and a "pull yourself together, Arabella, you are embarrassing the family" through gritted teeth. Bella wiped away the tears as she thought of her wonderful grandmother.

Her thoughts dwelled for a little while on her father's mother, a kind soul by all accounts. As she was her father's mother, she had an altogether different temperament from anyone on her mother's side. Her thoughts now drifted to her father, Taylor, and the tears came fast and warm. She let them run freely down her cheeks. The only time she cried and felt like she had made a terrible mistake was when she thought of Daddy. A true gentleman in every way, he was tall and slender with a well-styled grey head of hair, a young looking man for his age who took care of his appearance and his health in equal measure. Everyone who met Taylor instantly loved him, he was charismatic and charming in any social setting, like it was a joy for him to be in your presence. However, when the party ended, he would retreat into himself and a cut glass tumbler of whiskey and the spark would go out. At home, Taylor was downtrodden, a shadow of his former self, a yes man, an "I cannot fight you anymore" man. Even the house staff talked about how he was treated so badly, but always out of earshot of Mother. Apparently, Claudette knew best for everyone, including Taylor.

Bella thought about her return home after she had finished boarding school. Home – or the manor house as it was affectionately referred to by her friends – was a mid-century nine-bedroom house on a twelve-acre estate with imposing driveway, stables with manège, a tennis court, heated pool and a garage, which had been converted to a gym for the children to work out. The house itself was old and run down but the history in those walls was priceless. the interior by all accounts was, as would be expected, immaculate. It was almost showhome-like, nothing out of place; stunning light fittings and windows swathed in

143

the most sumptuous fabrics, colour coordinated bedrooms and en suites, an open fire in the main sitting room, family photos and well placed equestrian magazines, board games and a pack of cards all strategically placed to make any visitor fall under the illusion that this was a fun and loving family who loved to spend time together in this beautiful space. Images of mother and daughter laughing on the sofa together browsing the latest magazines whilst father and son played gin rummy was how the picture was to unfold to the untrained eye. The truth was it was all a façade that hid the fact that the house was a money pit of endless repairs and maintenance, which could not be left under any circumstances; what would the social circle think?

During the summer, Bella's parents set off on another trip, another holiday to talk about at the next social gathering, always having the upper hand on everyone else with tales of her latest trip with Daddy. So, there she was, no one there but the house staff to talk to, she held her breath until the anger that washed over her had subsided and then let her thoughts float to friends, only a couple of friends, the rest all wannabes. Once the house was empty, she had called on them to arrange the fastest trip out of there, so a quick turnaround then off to the airport to fly to Italy to meet up with her peers on a yacht off the Amalfi coast. As she sat in the back of the taxi, filled with mixed emotions of excitement and apprehension, Bella sent a quick text to her father to tell him her plans. Little did she know this would be her last contact with him.

Bella snapped selfies whilst she boarded the plane, champagne on the flight, it all had to be posted. Social media had crept in slowly but had now become a full time job for her, smiling her "look at my amazing life" smile, which she had practised and perfected over many lonely evenings in front of the mirror; not too showy because that wasn't who she was, but just enough to make people want to follow, want to see. What exotic destination you would be popping to with friends, what you would be wearing this autumn when you get back, what mist spray do you use on flights to make sure your skin stays hydrated, how many times do you work out, which designer's shoes are you wearing, who are you dating at the moment, do you have someone to prepare your food for you, whose make up do you use, do you take slimming pills…

The followers were so important to her and the numbers were growing, her own little army of followers hanging on every post, they built up her ever-so-lacking self-esteem and made her feel good, feel worthy, feel validated. She had all these followers and did not have to give anything back in return. It suited her awkward social personality. *They only know what I want them to see, they don't see my flaws, my unmade-up face in the morning, my deep lack of self-worth and self-esteem and my constant questioning of my mother's love for me.* They see holidays and shoes and champagne and lunch with friends. They see staged selfies of well-toned stomachs sucked in, bums and boobs out in "hot summer yacht poses" taken over and over again until the right shot can be posted once it had been touched up with filters for facial lines and red eye. They see her trying to fit in.

The trip on a friend's yacht should have been a welcome relief from everything, just time hanging out and having fun, then showing her followers who she was spending her time with, champagne on tap and the best food you could have only dreamt about. At this point in her daydreaming, her stomach rumbled so hard she doubled up in pain, but took some deep breaths, closed her eyes again and continued retracing the steps that led her here.

Yes, social media was full on, and it made Bella feel amazing and validated her life to herself, but it had a dark and dangerous side too, and the cracks in her confidence had started to spread like a cancer, making her second guess every post, every filter used, the trolls, oh my God the trolls were relentless with their taunting, and it appeared that the more popular she became the more of them followed her, like lemmings. She would block them and report them, but they would always find a way to get to her, commenting on everything she posted. But she had to post, her followers needed her, surely they needed to see her daily. If her posts started to dwindle, her followers might move onto someone else, and then what! They want to see her, and she needed their approval and their love more than she imagined.

But the responses kept coming.

You're ugly, you're so fat, do you know that no one loves you, all your friends hate you, why are you wearing that it makes you look terrible, you are showing off because your parents have money, I hope you die, you should do everyone a favour and kill yourself... no one would miss you.

She could cope with it on good days but on bad days she felt the velvet cloak of misery and doom shroud her every movement and every thought; what could she do to make them love her, why did they say these things? They didn't know her, they knew nothing of her insecurities, she was a kind, loving young lady who just wanted love in return. Bella knew that she could turn her phone off at the end of each day and not give them another thought, but the anxiety would build and build as morning came around, wondering what they would say to her that day; it was like boarding school all over again.

It wasn't until trolls started stalking her Mayfair apartment that true terror washed over her. She was not hurting anyone with her posts, it was all fun and good humour, she was never the sort of girl who would be unkind to anyone, never mind post that on social media! She just wanted to be loved and to fit in with her friends and their social medial accounts, not to always be the odd one out, the social misfit of her group; God, she just wanted to be popular. A kind, well-educated girl caught up in the twenty-first century social media phenomenon, just to fit in. Notes were pushed under the apartment block front doors addressed to her, all in the same vein. It was all too much, all too close to home, and she needed to escape to get away from it all, escape from her former life and start again somewhere new and to be invisible. Bella knew if she had gone home to discuss her fears, the family would tell her "don't be so silly and sensitive, Bella". Hugo would laugh at her. And her friends? Well, there was no one to talk to in the social circle because these were the friends who were so self-absorbed in their own social media world they couldn't care less. Finally she snapped. There was only one thing for it, she switched her phone off for the last time.

"Excuse me, young lady." The voice tore Bella from her daydreaming. Her eyes wide and bloodshot focused on the soft features of the police officer staring down at her, her warm brown eyes filled with concern. She had to think quickly, why was she here? What plausible excuse could she give? Her heart beating so hard in her chest, she was sure it was going to burst. She cleared her throat and spoke in her beautiful eloquent voice.

"Oh gosh, officer, I'm so sorry." Bella spoke slowly and breathed deeply so as not to look alarmed. "I must have fallen asleep here last night after a party."

"You don't look like you have been to a party," the officer replied, eyeing her up and down with a concerned look on her face. Shifting her gaze, she apologised profusely and promised the officer she would get a taxi straight back home and the officer smiled and said, "Make sure you are with a friend next time, you don't want to be on these streets at night by yourself."

Swiftly she collected her belongings, pushed them into the two bags she had and made her way through the park towards the bustling streets. Her daydream had meant she had missed the morning rush, the mist had lifted and there was a crisp bite to the day. She glanced behind her to check that the officer had gone, pulled up her collar to keep the cold air from her neck and, as she left the park, she walked past a weathered sign pinned to a wooden post, not noticing the somewhat faded print and the corners curling towards the pins holding it in place:

Have you seen our daughter, missing but hopefully still in the London area. Please call us, we are desperate.

★★★

Eve Wallace is a mum and interior and kitchen designer. When she was younger, her dad made up stories for her and she always hoped that one day she would be able to write a fictional story of her own. After meeting Jen at Fuzzy Flamingo she was inspired to get creative and her story writing journey began.

You can find out more about Eve here:
https://www.instagram.com/evewallacedesigns/

SEATED TOGETHER

Natalie Kyne-Dinsdale

Tears were flowing uncontrollably down his face when he realised that she had disappeared from his world for a second time. The pain of his heart breaking all over again was unbearable.

★

On a lovely sunny March morning, the powerful ray of light was beaming down and shining through Hayden's car windscreen. Although it was an icy cold day, the sun had helped the car to feel warm and snug.

Hayden was making his way down the narrow country lanes to get to the next village, as he was on his way to collect birthday gifts for his wife Emmi. Her birthday was two days away and he was trying to make it as special as he could, which was going to prove extremely difficult compared to all the other years they had celebrated together.

This birthday was Emmi's first birthday that she was

feeling heartbroken and completely lost without her treasured daughter to help them celebrate. The past six months had been the hardest time in her life. How would she ever move on from this? He knew she wouldn't want to celebrate but he wanted to do something, just the two of them.

Hayden was a kind and gentle man. His heart had also been torn apart, but he felt that they needed to do something where they could mark the occasion and feel like their daughter was spiritually with them too. He wasn't exactly sure how to do this, but he was off to search for some inspiration.

The day prior to this, after six months of trying to find answers, an inquest had found that their daughter was driving a stolen car when she died, and it appeared that she had crashed it into a ditch six miles away.

The outcome of the inquest had devastated the whole family. They were already grieving for the loss of their beautiful Olivia, and now they would never understand why she had stolen a car on her own. They had also lost hope of ever finding the answers, which they believed only she would know.

Had she been struggling with her college work? Maybe it was a cry for help that they had completely missed. Maybe she had been looking for attention. Hayden and Emmi had both been preoccupied with work, so they hadn't noticed any change in her.

So many questions but she was grievously no longer here to ask.

While Hayden was driving, he was thinking about the

inquest and still searching for answers, while also telling himself, "You just need to let it go now! You can't change what happened!"

Suddenly, an enormous *CRASH*!

"AAAHHHH! WHAT WAS THAT?!" shouted Hayden.

He opened his eyes and noticed that he was facing towards the side of the road and there was a pain in his head. He had no idea what had just happened!

A few seconds later, a panicked lady was tapping on his car window.

"Are you okay? Hey, are you okay?"

Hayden checked himself and it seemed to be a slight knock to his head. His heart was racing so fast, it felt like it was jumping out of his chest and he was confused and shaken.

The concerned lady opened his car door.

"I saw it all from my house, just there."

She pointed to a quaint little white cottage with a long stepping-stone pathway.

"Your car caught the edge of that wall, which is hidden amongst the bushes.

Hayden remembered then that the sun had been shining up from the road surface, and it was hard to see anything, but there was a stronger glare just as the crash happened.

"Please come in to call someone. Maybe you can be checked over before you drive anywhere!"

Hayden was so shaken he really wasn't ready to drive just yet, so he accepted. He was grateful for this stranger's kindness.

As they stepped into the cottage, she offered for him to take a seat. Hayden noticed four single chairs, all with different nature patterns on. Three were covered in a pink blossom print and one of them had a leaf print. He was drawn to sit in the odd one out, while the lady went to put the kettle on.

As Hayden sat in the chair, it really softened to him and he, almost immediately, felt goosebumps down the back of his neck.

While he was on his own, he rested his head back and took a few deep breaths to try and calm his shaking hands.

Suddenly...

"Dad! Dad! Please say you believe me! I wasn't driving! I was NOT driving! Please believe me!"

WHAT? Hayden thought.

He jumped up from the chair, but he couldn't hear her voice anymore. He was totally startled and completely confused with what was happening, but he wanted to see if he could get her to talk to him some more. He uneasily sat back down, rested his head back and closed his eyes, as he had done previously.

"Dad!" It sounded like Olivia's voice.

"Olivia? Is that you? What is happening?" he begged, desperate to work out what was going on.

Olivia was back here with him at this moment, and he could see her. Was he dreaming? She seemed so real right now.

Olivia spoke again. "Dad, I need to tell you! As I was walking down the road, I remember that something hit me hard. I also saw a man lift me into the driver's seat. There was nothing I could do, Dad! I just needed you to know! I was just walking, trying to get home. I love you and Mum very much!"

Hayden jumped up to try to reach out to his daughter, but just as quickly as she appeared, she had gone! He was back in the room, alone. Tears were flowing uncontrollably down his face when he realised that she had disappeared from his world for a second time. The pain of his heart breaking all over again was unbearable.

The lady returned with two cups of tea, and handed one to Hayden. She saw his tears and noticed that he was looking quite pale. She was very concerned.

"Is everything okay? I am so sorry, but I couldn't hear very well from the kitchen. I'll call for a doctor!"

He moved to a different chair while shakily taking the cup of tea. He took one sip of the piping hot tea and then made an excuse to leave. He couldn't make sense of anything and couldn't explain to her as he didn't understand it all himself.

He said he had to go and left hastily, jumped in his car and started driving home to see Emmi. Suddenly, something made him stop in his tracks and pull over. "I need to go back and get some more answers, to work out what was going on. I can't leave it like this!"

He turned around and drove back to the lady's house.

He jumped out of the car and knocked on the door! As the door opened, Hayden hurriedly said, "Excuse me! I am really sorry, but I need to ask you something!"

"Yes, of course!" she said, looking concerned.

"I wondered if I could please try something. I am really sorry, I never asked your name. I am Hayden."

"Ahh yes, I am Rose. I would like to help if I can."

"This is going to sound strange, and I couldn't explain earlier, but I felt a really strong presence from my daughter when I sat in your armchair." Hayden gestured towards the one with the leaves printed on it.

"I have never believed in spirits or ghosts, but she was definitely here. Would you mind if I tried again? To see if it happens again?"

"Oh my goodness! Yes, of course! It really is a unique chair. I bought it from an antique auction over fifty years ago and reupholstered it. I have never told anyone this, but my late husband used to visit me when he first passed away, eight years ago. I had great comfort in talking to him many nights for a number of years. Gradually it became less frequent and now I find it hard to sit there. I was just waiting for him for longer each time. I think he had found his peaceful place and needed to leave." Rose had gone into a daze thinking about how much she missed him. "You are very welcome to try again. I shall leave you on your own to feel more relaxed, as it is an extremely emotional experience."

Hayden was thankful to Rose and walked over to the chair. He was hesitant about sitting down. It was all so surreal and yet comforting at the same time.

He sat down and he felt the same gentle tingly feeling he felt earlier. He rested his head back into the chair and closed his eyes, really hoping to see – or even just hear – Olivia again.

Nothing happened! He opened one eye. Still nothing!

He closed both eyes again, took a deep breath to try to relax, then he heard...

"Dad, I need you to know! I never wanted to leave you and Mum. Tell Mum it is okay. I am safe and I can see you both. Please find a way to be happy again!"

Once again, the tears were streaming down Hayden's face. He called out, "Olivia! Olivia!" but she was no longer there.

He sat forward and held his head in his hands. This felt like a final goodbye, but a tremendous weight had lifted. He was obviously still missing Olivia, but he had some comfort in knowing the truth.

Hayden and Rose spoke for a while before he went home. He felt strangely fortunate to have crashed right here outside Rose's cottage and he explained how grateful he was to her for everything.

He had thought of an idea for Emmi's birthday and was excited to get things in place.

Hayden arrived back in their village and, although it was raining, the sun was shining, and he spotted an incredible rainbow in the sky ahead of him.

The morning of Emmi's birthday arrived. She found it extremely hard to get out of bed any day over the past six months but this was going to be an even harder day.

Hayden knew it was going to be a struggle to persuade Emmi to get up, but he really wanted her to receive her precious gift, even though he was utterly anxious about how she would feel. He persuaded her eventually to have breakfast together. Thankfully, he was able to guide her into the living room first.

Right in front of the bay window, she saw a lovely armchair. However, Emmi was confused. "That's lovely, honey, but we already have enough chairs in this room!"

Hayden sat Emmi down to explain everything that had happened over the past two days. She couldn't believe what she was hearing, and she had so many questions. They cried, laughed, reminisced and cried some more.

Hayden had been able to get the armchair delivered from Rose's house early in the morning, while Emmi was still sleeping. The last time he went into Rose's house, she had insisted that he took the chair as she no longer needed it and felt it would be comforting for them both right now.

The armchair, which they realised was covered with an olive leaf print material, was lovely in their front room. Olivia's closest friend, their dog, Tully, made it his new home.

When they wanted to feel close to Olivia, they would sit in the chair and cuddle Tully. She never appeared again to them, not to talk to anyway, but they could feel her presence with them always, especially when they were seated together.

★★★

Natalie Kyne-Dinsdale is a qualified fitness instructor and Irish dance coach. She loves to help children and adults to improve their mental and physical health with Irish Dance, Fitness, Mindset and Forever Aloe Vera based products. She also loves to help small businesses with branding and various design work, after 20 years in her graphic design career.

Irish Dance & Fitness: www.facebook.com/hackettkyne
Forever Aloe Vera and Health Supplements: www.
facebook.com/alwayskindandbeautiful
Graphic Design: www.facebook.com/
iolitedesignandartstudio

NESSIE

Raychel Paterson

In the conservatory, George lies prone on a faded wicker recliner that creaks with every movement of his withering frame. Today's lunch – Christmas leftovers – was finally finished with. Agnes listens to his contented snoring. It used to be his habit to nap for at least an hour after a Sunday lunch. Now he sleeps every day after every meal, be it breakfast, lunch, or supper. She cuts his food up to feed him by hand. It's as if he were a baby again. She has been running on autopilot since he was diagnosed five long years ago. Years of waiting; watching, almost grieving the loss of how life used to be. No life at all really. There was always the forlorn hope of any improvements, however slight, being a sign that he was getting better. Shallow smiles and dipped heads the only open signs that people knew without saying that life was half a prison sentence for the both of them. Agnes had learned, especially with company – in the early days – how to keep half an ear cocked for the slightest groan or sudden movement to indicate that he was awake.

Today it's Boxing Day. George has been positively beaming, watching snow fall lightly on the bare arms of the elm trees.

"Ness?" He pointed a quivering finger…

"Yes, darling. It's snow! Isn't it beautiful?"

He'd moved his hand skyward and began to wave, as if to welcome each individual snowflake by name as they floated slowly earthward.

"Yeah," he managed to say before his arm fell heavily into his lap. He sighed, then closed his eyes.

Agnes moved as quickly around her tiny kitchen as her arthritis and her husband's awareness on any particular day would allow. By rote, she cleaned pots and bone china that didn't need cleaning. On her way into the lounge, she began a routine long ago learned at the side of her elder brother that included much checking and placement of objects that, for the most part, just didn't need checking or placement. There were no ghosts or mischievous spirits moving furniture at the dead of night in *this* house. Well. At least not yet. She shivered despite herself. Why was she having thoughts and feelings like this? For *GOD's* sake!! He's still here in the next room snoring fit to burst. Instantly feeling guilty for harbouring such thoughts, she embraced herself. It was a poor replacement for the intimacy they'd once shared when even the tiniest of plans went awry or, in all the rushing about, a keepsake had been accidentally broken or lost. She'd get frustrated and *hormonal*, being the first to berate George as if it were solely *his* fault for *her* shortcomings.

Agnes swished an old-fashioned feather duster over

160

wooden picture frames. Indulgently, she gazed at the old black and white photographs of their marriage. George looked particularly resplendent and handsome in his new RAF pilot officer's uniform, with his new bride on his arm. She'd had to let Sadie in on her "little secret" of being "late", before divulging that she was marrying *her* George and needed a dress running up as quickly as possible the following day. The pictures showed the two of them on a wonderful spring afternoon standing outside the registry. Nessie, as George began to call her, wearing a full-length ivory and gold brocade dress. She always said that their wedding had been spectacularly unplanned, from the hurriedly arranged registrar to the soldiers who, while on home leave for a long weekend, had acted as witnesses for the price of a pint of beer or two. Agnes remembered that they had already had a skinful anyway. She smiled ruefully at the memories. There were snaps of both of them taken some months later proudly showing off baby Cathie. Such a happy time. She smiled. Agnes sighed, wistfully shaking her head.

Oh Cath, darling. I wish you'd come back to us…to me.

Cathie used to visit regularly. She was the only one who could legally drive a car, so forsaking her own family for a few hours a week to help out with little jobs for her parents around their house was a natural thing to do; shopping and taking in her parents' washing as a favour. Their own washer had seen better days but George had lost all interest and the abilities to fix most things in the house. Growing ever grumpy and frustrated with himself, everyone walked on eggshells. It had only been a matter of time before the atmosphere had grown toxic.

Two weeks earlier

Inevitably, the day came that they had all been dreading, it crept up on them. A day like any other. Dull and overcast outside, the winter season had just found out it had a purpose and blew out some experimental winds along the coast. Just enough to cause annoyance if you hadn't gone out wearing an extra layer of clothes or a scarf.

George had been staring out at the back garden from his recliner in the conservatory. He was wearing a thicker than usual cardigan that boasted leather patches on the sleeves. Sweating profusely, he levered himself into a sitting position before grabbing hold of his cane and launching himself at the conservatory doors in what he must have thought was a fluid movement of perfect hand/eye co-ordination and looking anything but. There were shouts of "Dad! George!! Oh GOD look out!!" from Cathie, Nessie and the washing machine repairman, but not in that particular order.

Warnings of imminent danger can have one or two immediate effects on the person in danger. Ordinarily – with his military survival instincts and youthfulness on his side –George would have rolled onto his padded shoulder and an arm to protect his head from banging against the Perspex of the door. On hearing Cathie scream, he turned his attention to her and what she was doing before anyone else, believing she was in danger. George, distracted, banged his head on the Perspex and had an instant before he lost consciousness. Time enough to register a woman he didn't recognise removing an envelope from the safe where all the valuables and cash were kept.

Although it wasn't her fault, Cathie decided not to visit her dad for a while, as it became painfully obvious that he didn't trust her. She had visited a few days after his fall and he'd stared unblinkingly at her as a cat would a bird in a tree. There was no recognition of his only child anymore. She'd run, blinded by tears, as her father, brandishing his cane, had tried to get out of his seat, screaming, "Get out! Nessie! Call the police. She's trying to steal our money. Go on, get out before I kill you myself! Bitch!" he spat.

Cathie was inconsolable. Try as Agnes might, the bond between father and daughter was as strong as their own relationship. Cathie refused to see her dad as anything but a hero in her eyes. She *needed* to make him see that... that she loved him more than anything. Her tears threatened to well up... Agnes' hands tightened slightly on her daughters'. "Cathie. Sweetheart. He knows. Daddy already knows."

After that, Agnes' days and nights had, almost without her noticing, merged into one endless round of dusting, sweeping and – because the washer was left broken waiting for a new belt, care of the repair man – washing filthy soiled clothes by hand. She makes sure George is clean and comfortable before pouring herself a chilled can of Guinness, a tonic the doctor had okayed for her because of its iron content. She'd promised herself and the local GP – Doctor Singh... lovely man, very sympathetic – that she'd try to take things a little easier. To that end, she sat, relaxing as best she could, whenever she could, not very often allowing herself the luxury of reminiscing...

...Was it the hacking cough or the plasticky sound of

an empty beaker on hard tile that pricked her ears first? Agnes was at her husband's side within seconds. His good arm had caught the beaker of water that she'd used with his medication… except… she didn't give him all the meds earlier. She couldn't have. There… on the tiled floor near the rug. The yellow pill. The one that helps him sleep.

Oh dear lord, I must have gone to sleep. What was I thinking? How could I have been so selfish?

His hands slapped at the unseen moth of her arms, hers pinning his down to stop him hurting himself further.

"Please, please stop it, darling. Please. Please stop," she sobbed.

Even as she held his venous wrists to her breasts as tightly as she could, she felt her own strength falling away. George was still physically strong and her body shook with the effort of trying to control him. Breathless minutes later, his spasms had eased enough for her to try to administer the medication properly this time. Agnes watched to make sure it was calming him, giving him peace once again.

But for how long? she thought. *How long this time?*

"I went to sleep. What was I thinking? You stupid, stupid woman. Cathie would never forgive me if I'd… what? Let him die? All for the sake of reminiscing!"

Agnes was shocked. Realising that she'd spoken out loud, she covered her mouth with long, age-mottled fingers, looking guiltily at him. He showed no signs whatever of having heard.

"You wouldn't understand, anyway, would you? Not really. You haven't heard what I've been saying to you for years, George. Have you?" she whispered. Holding him down had sapped her strength and the effort to stand herself upright sent a dagger of pain through her weakened legs. Grimacing, she edged slowly to her feet and shuffled slowly through the kitchen, constantly eyeing her husband for further signs of movement. He was still. Regaining her strength, she strode purposely to the refrigerator, popped the cans of Guinness and poured them down the sink.

Reaching deep into the pocket of her housecoat for the "special" key that nobody else knew about, she felt its familiar shape in her hand, then moved decisively into the lounge. Agnes inserted the key carefully into the old oak writing bureau and turned it in the lock. With her senses heightened, the click of the key sounded like a thunderclap. Behind a collection of letters and postcards, a cardboard shoebox lay in front of her, still looking as if it may contain shoes. It was anything but. Removing the lid, she folded back the oil cloth inside to reveal George's old Webley revolver. The stale oily smell made her retch. She looked at the hated object. They'd had huge arguments over it being kept in the home at all.

"What if Cathie finds it?"

"She won't, I'll lock it up."

"No, George, I won't have it in the house! It's dangerous."

But she'd relented and he had locked it away, but knowing it was there had caused the first real strain on their marriage.

She hesitantly picked it up by its embossed handle. Its unfamiliar weight more than she expected.

I'm sorry, George, sweetheart. I can't take any more of this. I'm just so tired.

Agnes walked the longest walk of her life. Past the wedding photos and their baby girl.

My life's just memories now.

Past the broken beltless washer, to where the kitchen became the conservatory. She held the gun quivering at her side. Tears dried instantly on her face as she faltered behind her husband.

"Mum. I'm sorry," said Cathy. She held a bouquet of roses.

"I got your message, sweetheart. Oh, they're lovely, really. There's a vase by the window."

"The back door was open, so I let myself in. Here's that part you needed for the washer. It should…"

Cathy's smile faded as her eyes scanned down.

"Mum? What on earth?"

"It's okay, darling, it doesn't work."

"But what were you…?"

"Oh! Love, you wouldn't believe the arguments I had with Dad over this. After he got demmobed he borrowed it from the RAF as a souvenir. He wanted to keep it for 'our protection'. When you came along, I didn't want it in the house. You know? In case you found it growing up. I compromised with Dad, though. Kept it safe but had the firing pin removed without telling him. Looking back, it's bloody lucky we didn't need it, eh?"

"So, what you doing with it now, Mum?"

"Well, love, I'm showing it to you… See, no firing pin, no registration numbers, no bullets in the chamber and none up the spout. That's a proper saying from the old days. I had 'one up the spout' when I was pregnant with you. Ha ha. Anyway, another reason I'm telling you is that if Dad gets a sudden brainstorm and he remembers where the gun is, you'll be able to tell him it isn't there anymore. But you know I don't think it's likely now, do you?"

"No. Mum?"

"What?"

"Thanks!"

"You put those flowers in water. I'll make the tea."

★★★

Raychel lives a mere stone's throw from Ken Follett and used to pass Barbara Cartland's cottage on her way home from work. Not that she is as prolific as either.

She has had some micro-fiction pieces (100 words a shot) as well as a "taster" memoir chapter published on the Net. This, now, is uncharted territory, which marks a stuttering effort to increase her fictional word count. and is scoping a story aimed at the younger end of the Disney age market.

Raychel can normally be found on:
https://www.facebook.com/rayCH.paterson/
It's her weapon of choice.

NEW BEGINNINGS

Sally Sarson

As the last of the snow cleared, Hannah looked out of her bedroom window and wished for better things to come.

It was January, the bleakest month of the year; the December festivities were over, the Christmas cheer long gone, and she was left all alone, in her flat, all by herself.

Things had changed so much over the last year. Actually, everything had changed since the accident. That fateful day when her life had changed forever.

She wiped a tear from her cheek and turned away from the window. It was time to start over, it was time to look forward and make plans. Unlucky in love, her mum had always said, but when she'd found James she knew she'd found herself that special someone, someone to share her darkest days with, someone to lift her up no matter what and who could make her laugh even when she was in a terrible mood.

Everything was going so perfectly, they were saving for a much bigger place. They'd seen the one they wanted, it was a four-bed semi with a huge garden for their future kids to run around in, a big garage for James to tinker away in and a separate study where Hannah could work on her paintings and store all of her much-loved books.

They were madly in love, her heart had always soared when she was with him. They had the most intense connection and one of them would often say out loud what the other was thinking, their bodies falling into a natural rhythm when they were together, often mirroring each other's stances without even noticing.

That was until that fateful day in June, nearly eighteen months ago now, the day that would change her life forever. It had been a warm summer's day and James had been itching to go out on his motorbike and "tear up" the roads, as he always joked. Hannah had been too busy with work to be able to join him, so he'd gone out on his own, something that she'd never forgive herself for.

The lorry that struck him hadn't seen him. The driver said that he'd come out of nowhere. James hadn't stood a chance, the lorry had hit him head on and he'd been killed instantly.

Pain ripped through Hannah's heart as she remembered the police turning up on her doorstep. James didn't have any family; she was his only next of kin. The moment she had opened the door to them, she knew what they were going to say, she knew they were going to tell her that her James had gone.

They say time is a great healer and that may well be true, but for Hannah something inside of her had died that day too. On her darkest of days, she wished that she had been with him, that she hadn't let him go alone; then they would have both been taken and she wouldn't have to feel the heartache of life without him.

Hannah's friends had been so supportive since the accident, her two sisters were constantly by her side and always checking in with her, inviting her around to their houses for tea and Sunday lunches. She had spent this last Christmas with her eldest sister Jo, her husband and three kids. She had a wonderful time, but there was always that forever loneliness deep down in her heart, a piece of her that was missing.

Hannah let out a sigh and shivered slightly. Her flat was cold and she grabbed her favourite jumper; it was one of James' old jumpers actually, he'd leant it to her on their first date and she'd never given it back.

She looked at the boxes around her; it was time to move on, a fresh new start. A new town, a new job in a new art gallery and hopefully a fresh new outlook on life.

Hannah had decided before Christmas that she needed to leave the flat, there were too many painful memories for her. Everywhere she looked she could see James, he'd be slouched on the sofa watching TV, or in the kitchen cooking her favourite food. She'd applied for the role on a whim, really, and she couldn't believe her luck when her application had been accepted. She hadn't been down for a face-to-face interview, everything had been sorted over the phone. Mark, the owner of the gallery, was keen to hand over the business to someone young with fresh ideas and the fact that she herself was an artist was the icing on the cake, or so he put it.

Yes, it was time to leave life behind as she knew it, she needed to leave the past behind her. James would always be with her, deep inside her heart, but she felt the time had come, the need for change was upon her and she felt ready.

Her friends thought she was crazy. She was moving from the wet and rainy East Midlands and heading down the southwest to St Ives in Cornwall. It was a place she had spent many holidays as a child and she had such fond memories of playing on the beach with her father and building sandcastles. Later on in life, she had visited and spent hours laying on the beach, reading her favourite books and looking out to sea. Cornwall was to be her new start in life.

Packing up all of her belongings had been easy; clothes, books, photographs, that was about it. She had sold the flat to one of her friends and was selling it fully furnished, leaving everything else behind right down to the sofa she had chosen with James and the curtains that they'd hung in their bedroom the very first night they had moved in.

She smiled at the memory of James saying they didn't need curtains up, that it would be nice to wake up to the natural light beaming through the bedroom window. Hannah had laughed and had reminded him of the nosy neighbour across the road who only shut his curtains when he went to bed; did they really want to be giving him an eyeful every time they got undressed? James had simply winked at her and told her she'd have to get undressed in the bathroom as her naked body was for his viewing pleasure only.

The hardest thing had been sorting through James'

stuff; she had wanted to keep hold of everything. She liked the sight of his trainers next to the front door, even though it had driven her crazy whilst he was alive as she had been forever tripping over the damn things. His trainers at the front door to the flat and his jacket casually thrown over the back of the sofa had always indicated to her that he was home. It gave her comfort and she had left them there for months after the funeral.

As she stuffed the last of her shoes into the holdall, she stood up and took one final last look around the flat. She glanced at the clock on the wall, it was 8am, it was just starting to get light, and it was time she hit the road.

It was New Year's Day, there wouldn't be much traffic on the road, but she wanted to set off to give her plenty of time for the long journey ahead. Her friends had begged her to stay for a few more days, but she was adamant that today was as good as any to make her trip, and that besides, her new role started next week, and she wanted to make sure she was fully settled.

The gallery was only a small shop, but it also came with a one-bedroom fully furnished flat above that she could live in rent free as part of her salary. The art gallery promoted local artists' work and Hannah was permitted to display her own artwork in the shop too. Not that she had done much over the past year. Since James' death she had hardly picked up a paintbrush and she was hoping this new start would help to inspire her and reignite her passion for painting.

She grabbed her car keys and her holdall and took one last look around the flat, before she shut the door firmly behind her and headed down towards her car. Tears rolled down her cheeks, she knew she was making the right move, but it was tearing her heart in two leaving all the memories of James behind.

She threw her holdall onto the back seat of her red Fiesta, which was already crammed full of her belongings. She sincerely hoped she would make the journey down to Cornwall without any issues; her trusty red Fiesta had been hers for four years now and hadn't once let her down, lovingly serviced every year, passing every MOT with flying colours. James had always poked fun at her car, saying she needed something more sporty and with more room, but Hannah loved that car, it was cheap motoring and would be perfect for the winding tight roads of St Ives.

Hannah fired up the engine and turned the heaters up. It was a chilly morning, and her car didn't have the luxury of heated seats. She tapped the St Ives postcode into her satnav and waited for it to load the directions. Four hours and fifty-nine minutes it said. This, of course, didn't take into account the stop she would take at Exeter services. Hannah reckoned she'd be in St Ives by about 3pm if the journey went well.

*

Six hours later, an exhausted Hannah pulled into the harbour in St Ives. The drive had been a lonely one with just the radio to keep her company. The harbour was deserted apart from a few seagulls sitting staggered across the harbour wall. She had arranged to meet Mark, the owner of the gallery, on the harbour front near the fish and chip shop on the corner. As she drove round down the road slowly, she spotted a middle-aged man standing outside the chip shop wearing a big coat, bobble hat and gloves. He waved at Hannah as she pulled up next to the pavement. Hannah stretched, turned off the engine and grabbed her coat and scarf from the passenger seat and stepped out of her car.

"Well hello there," Mark bellowed, his voice deep and his smile spread across his face. He held out a hand to Hannah for her to shake.

"Hello, you must be Mark, it's lovely to finally meet you," she replied, shaking his hand and feeling shy all of a sudden. Wrapping her scarf around her neck, she shivered; it was so cold out here compared to the warmth of her car.

"Pleasant journey?" he asked. "The gallery is just down here, follow me. I'll give you a quick tour and then we'll head on up to the flat and get you all settled in. You must be exhausted after your long drive. Have you eaten?" He turned to look at Hannah.

"Err, yes, thank you," she replied. "I grabbed a sandwich and drink at Exeter services, so I'm all good."

"Good good, well there's not a lot open today with it being New Year's Day and all, but the pub just down the road is open until 8pm tonight and they do lovely home cooked food if you fancy anything later," he replied warmly. They walked a few steps. "Right, here we are then." Mark gestured to the shop front just a few steps down from where she had parked. The window frame was painted white and there were lots of coastal paintings displayed in the window.

"It looks lovely," replied Hannah, eager to get inside and away from the chilly coastal wind.

He held up a set of keys. "The small key is for the Yale lock for this front door and the large key is for the back door right out the back of the shop. There's no alarm or anything to worry about, we all look out for each other around here." Mark smiled as he unlocked the door with ease and they both stepped inside.

Hannah, pleased to be out of the wind, loosened off her scarf and did a quick scan of the shop; paintings hung along the back wall, there were small hand painted gift items and some small jewellery items in a white cabinet just next to the window. There were two tables inside, a medium-sized counter with a till and what looked like a huge coffee machine and some freshly baked muffins in a cake stand towards the end of it. This took Hannah by surprise; she wasn't aware she was required to serve coffee too.

Hannah glanced at Mark who had already spotted the worried look across her face. "Now then, there's been a slight change to the plan. My son has decided that we as a business needed to offer the customers something more. Out of season, the shop isn't as busy, as I explained to you over the phone, but we want to cater to the needs of our locals, so he decided it would be a good idea to offer coffee and cakes to either sit in or take away. It encourages people into the shop and, whilst they are waiting, they can take a look around. Don't worry, though, he will give you full training on the coffee machine and the cakes are delivered fresh every day from the bakery just up the road. He'll be on hand here with you every day for your first few weeks to help you get settled. I hope that's okay with you?" Mark was looking at her, awaiting her response.

"Yes, that's fine with me." What else could she say? "I mean, I guess it makes sense and helps to bring in some additional income for the business, which is always a bonus," she added, not wanting Mark to see how uncomfortable she was with the idea.

"Yes, that's the plan, it will also help you to get to know the locals a lot better, which will hopefully make you feel more at home. Right then, shall we head on up to the flat and get you settled in?" Mark gestured to the back door and Hannah followed him through.

"The entrance to the flat is just up those stairs," Mark said with a nod of his head as he locked the shop door behind him. Hannah glanced up the stone steps to the cute pastel blue door at the top of the steps. There was a holly wreath hung on the door knocker just above the letterbox.

"That was the wife's idea," said Mark as he saw Hannah gazing up at the door.

"It looks lovely, thank you," she replied.

"Right you are then, here's the key, you go and let yourself in and I'll be up in a sec, I've forgotten to lock the front door to the shop. Sheila will play hell with me if she knows that I have left it unlocked again," Mark said, rolling his eyes. "She thinks I'm losing my marbles as it is, don't want to give her any further ammunition," he said, turning back to the shop door.

Hannah stifled a small giggle and headed up the steps to her new home. The front door was so pretty and there was a small window just to the left-hand side of the door with a window basket full of gorgeous, colourful flowers.

She took the key and slid it into the lock and turned the handle. She pushed the door open gently and stepped inside. The warmth of the flat hit her and she felt instantly at ease. There was a coat stand with an umbrella to the right of her and a small corridor in front. She pushed the door to, not wanting to shut it completely. She took off her coat and hung it on the stand. Her trainers came off next and she let her feet sink into the luxurious fluffy grey carpet under them. To the left of her was a door, which was her bedroom, a big double bed dressed with a pastel blue duvet set and a coastal picture of the sea hanging above it, a wooden bedside table with a reading lamp and a huge wooden chest of drawers to the right-hand side.

She carried on down the little corridor, which brought her out into an open plan lounge with a small kitchen attached. There was a cute breakfast bar setting the kitchen and lounge apart with two wooden barstools against it.

The lounge had a two-seater sofa with a big fur throw thrown over the back, facing the big bay window looking out over the harbour. Hannah stood for a moment taking in the scenery below. The harbour stretched out in front of her, she could see the boats bobbing gently in the water and she could see her car parked just down the road. The view was perfect, and Hannah felt instantly at home.

She heard the door open and Mark called out to her. "Come in," she replied. Mark appeared behind her.

"Lovely view, isn't it?" he asked. "It's a view I never get tired of looking at."

"It's breathtaking," Hannah replied. "I can't thank you

enough for this opportunity, it really does mean the world to me. It's a brand new start and I won't let you down."

"You're more than welcome, Hannah, I hope you'll be very happy here. Now, where are your car keys? I'll go and grab your bags for you then you can park the car on the side street out back."

"Oh, its okay, I only have a few boxes and bags and I was going to grab them later. I was hoping to go for a walk along the beach before it gets dark, blow away the cobwebs and stretch my legs after the long journey."

"Oh, of course. Well, if you're sure, I'll leave you to it. I'll pop by tomorrow morning and check in on you, if that's okay?" Mark said, walking back to the door.

"That would be lovely, thank you." Hannah smiled at Mark as he left, closing the door gently behind him.

She grabbed her coat off the stand, wrapped her scarf back around her neck and slipped her trainers back on. She shut the door firmly behind her, dropping her keys into her pocket, and made her way back out on to the main road and headed for the beach.

It was awfully quiet as she walked down alongside the harbour wall, it was so different to the hustle and bustle of the town in peak season. She suspected that most of the locals where cosied up at home with their families, nursing their sore heads from the previous night's celebrations.

Just a short walk and Hannah had arrived at the beach, the sun starting to set and the waves gently hitting the shore. She was always mesmerised with how beautifully clear and blue the sea was down here, it was like being abroad somewhere. She walked along the shore, careful not to let the waves hit her trainers. Her wellies would have been more appropriate footwear but they were buried in the boot of her car amongst the rest of her belongings.

She let the thoughts of the past year run through her mind, a sea of endless lonely nights and long days at the gallery; she had worked long hours by choice, anything to delay going back to their flat. As for her personal life, her sister had set her up on a blind date a few months ago with a guy from her office. They had been out to dinner a few times, but Hannah's heart just wasn't in it; there was no spark and she needed to feel that connection if there was ever going to be anyone else.

Hannah was so deep in her thoughts that she didn't hear the man shout. All of a sudden, she was aware of her legs being swept out from underneath her as she lost her balance and fell backwards onto the wet sand. She lay there for a few seconds before attempting to get up.

"I am so sorry about that," said a man's voice. Hannah looked up at the man peering down at her. "Here, let me give you a hand up," he said, reaching out his hand so she could take it.

"No thank you," Hannah replied. "I'm perfectly capable of picking myself up, thank you very much," she huffed, as she pulled herself up onto her feet. Her jeans were wet from the sand and she was pretty sure the back of her hair was covered in sand too.

"I did try to warn you, but you were just standing, staring out to sea. It was my dog, Harris. He was chasing the seagulls and all of a sudden he was heading straight for you. I tried to call him back, but he doesn't listen, the stubborn old boy. Look, here he comes now." The man pointed to a stocky black Labrador that was bounding back up the beach towards them. "Here boy, c'mon," he called out, but the dog just carried on running past him in the opposite direction.

Hannah straightened up her jacket and looked the stranger straight in the eyes. "Well, if your dog doesn't listen – which he quite clearly doesn't! – may I suggest that you keep him on a lead? Especially when there are people about!"

"Hey look, no harm done, and you're right, he should be on a lead, but I figured there wouldn't be anyone down here today with it being New Year's Day and all. Look, I'm sorry, okay?" the stranger replied with a smile. He was taller than Hannah and she kept having to look up to meet his eyes. He was about her age, definitely a local, she reckoned, possibly a surfer maybe? He had a slim, athletic build.

"Apology accepted," Hannah replied. "Now, if you'll excuse me, I must be heading back." She turned and began to walk away from him.

"It was nice to meet you by the way!" he called out after her. Hannah turned around. "The name's Dan," he said. "Just in case you were wondering. Maybe I could take you out for a drink sometime?" he asked, smiling at her.

"I don't think so, I'm not in the habit of meeting strangers for drinks," she replied, and with that, she turned away from him and headed back up the beach.

"Well, if you change your mind, I'm usually down here the same time every night walking Harris," he called out after her. She shook her head. God, the cheek of him! How arrogant was he! She hoped all the locals weren't going to be as cocky as he was.

★

Hannah woke the next morning to the sound of the seagulls squawking just outside of her window. She yawned and stretched; she needed coffee. She swung her legs out of bed and walked barefoot to the kitchen. She flicked on the kettle and walked over to open the living room curtains. She was greeted with the view of the harbour, a few boats gently bobbing about on the sea. The sky was blue and there wasn't a cloud in sight. What a perfect way to start the day, she thought. A quick coffee and a shower and she'd be good to go.

Thirty minutes later, she was showered and dressed in her blue denim jeans and grey hoodie, her hair hanging wet around her shoulders, and she'd popped on some mascara and lip balm. No need to make an effort today, she wasn't planning on bumping into anyone.

She shut the door behind her and headed down the steps to the back entrance to the gallery, put the key in the lock and pushed the door open. Stepping inside, the shop was lovely and warm, and she worried she may overheat in her hoodie. The counter and till were just to the right of her, and the two tables were just in front. She'd already decided that she would move the tables closer to the window so that customers could sit and admire the view of the harbour. She also wanted to rearrange the artwork on the walls and move them around to give the gallery a fresh new feel.

After an hour, she had moved the tables, swapped the paintings around and was just about to start sorting out around the back of the counter when she heard a tap on the front door. She looked up and saw Mark standing there with a huge smile on his face. He was wrapped up in his big thick winter coat and bobble hat. Hannah smiled and went over to let him in.

"Morning Hannah, beautiful morning, isn't it? Woah you have been busy this morning! Eager to get started, are you? That's what I like to see!" Mark said as he stepped inside the shop and unbuttoned his coat. "I like what you've done with the place, it seems bigger somehow," he said, looking around. Hannah spotted him looking at the table that she had moved next to the window.

"I thought that a table next to the window would be nice. People can come and sit and relax, enjoy a coffee, whilst admiring the view. It also puts them in the eyeline for any new pieces that come in, as I will display them over here," Hannah said, pointing to the wall opposite.

"I love it! Just what this place needed, Hannah, a fresh set of eyes." Mark's face beamed as he took a seat at the window table. "Now, I mentioned last night about my son popping in next week to show you the ropes. I spoke with him earlier and he's free this morning, so he's going to swing by shortly and give you a run through on that coffee machine."

"That sounds great, Mark, thank you. Has he always been involved in the family business?" she asked, pulling up a seat next to Mark, grateful to take the weight off her feet for a short while.

"Only in the last nine months, really. He moved away up north when he got married, we hardly ever saw him, but it's been nice having him back home." Mark spotted the confused look on Hannah's face. "He split up with his wife last year. She was a nurse and he found out she'd been having an affair with one of the junior doctors where she worked, so he ended it, made her buy him out of the mortgage and he's moved back home with us for a while until he finds his own place. Think he's a bit lonely down here to be honest, not that he'd ever say. He spends a lot of time on his own out walking, just him and the dog." A look of sadness flicked across Mark's face.

"I'm sorry to hear that, it must have been a difficult time for you all, it's never easy when a relationship ends," Hannah replied.

"I'm sure he'll be fine once he gets a bit more settled. He's been on a couple of dates since he's been back, but nothing serious. Sheila's worried he'll end up living with us and never finding anyone else. I've told her not to be silly, of course, he just needs time to get over her and to get the divorce finalised. Once that's all sorted, he can wipe his hands of her for good." Mark looked up. "Speak of the devil, here he comes now." Mark smiled and put his hand up.

Hannah looked up and followed Mark's gaze to a man in a blue Barbour jacket and bobble hat, with a dog bounding around at his feet. Hannah's stomach dropped; it was the guy from the beach last night.

The man smiled and waved back, the dog straining to get off the lead and chase seagulls, pulling him, making him quicken his steps. He arrived at the shop and, before Hannah had barely opened the door, the dog managed to free himself, jumping up at the door, making it swing open. He barked and jumped up at Hannah, licking her face.

Mark stood up. "Hannah, this is my son Dan. Dan, I'd like you to meet Hannah, she's going to be running the gallery for us."

Dan held out his hand towards Hannah, a smile forming across his lips. "We meet again," he said. Hannah felt her face flush.

"Yes, it would appear so," she replied, wanting the ground to swallow her up.

A confused look formed across Mark's face. "Have you two met before?" he asked. Both Hannah and Dan looked awkwardly at each other. Meanwhile, Harris the dog was busy chewing the shoelace on Hannah's trainers.

Dan broke the silence. "Yes, Dad, Harris and I bumped into Hannah down on the beach last night. Harris is quite taken with her, he even swept her off her feet!" Hannah could feel her cheeks starting to redden as he spoke, the image of her lying flat on her back in the sand flashing before her eyes. God, what must he think of her? Dan must have spotted her discomfort, as he turned to Mark. "Dad, why don't you take Harris for a walk down the beach before he destroys Hannah's trainers and I'll stay here and show her the ropes?" It was more of a statement than a request and Mark, sensing the discomfort between them both, grabbed hold of Harris' lead and led him out of the shop.

As soon as the door closed, Dan took a step closer to

Hannah. "Look, I know we didn't exactly hit it off last night, but can we maybe start again?" Hannah was hesitant and then she remembered Mark's words about Dan and his wife, and she felt guilty for having been so rude to him down on the beach. It's not like he did it on purpose and he seemed like a nice normal guy now.

"Yes, I'd like that," she replied.

"Great!" A look of relief spread across Dan's face. "Right then," he said, unzipping his coat and draping it over one of the chairs. "Let's start over, shall we? Hi, my name's Dan, and I can make an excellent latte, shall we get started?" he asked, gesturing with his hand to the coffee machine. "Ladies first," he said. "And don't worry, I'm fully house trained and I promise I won't lick your face," he said, smiling. "Well, not unless you want me to, of course?" he added, a mischievous glint in his eye.

Hannah laughed. He was toying with her again and she was determined not to bite back. He was quite a character this one. The next few weeks were going to be very interesting indeed.

***

Sally lives in Leicestershire in the UK with her husband and two daughters. She has always had a passion for writing from an early age and this is her second piece of published work.

An avid reader, Sally can often be found with her head in a book and usually has two or three on the go at any one time. She loves to read all types of fiction with crime, thriller and romance at the top of her list.

Sally also runs her very own Etsy shop called SallyBee Design where she sells personalised handmade gifts for all occasions.

Sally can often be found hanging out over on Instagram, you can follow her: @sallybeedesigns

A MOMENT IN TIME

Sarah Lake

For a moment in time, she just sat there. She sat there watching the children playing in the shade of the shabbily erected gazebo, all totally absorbed in their make-believe world of fairies and giant gorillas; a truly curious mix. Four beautiful children, all made by her, all totally unique and all playing together in an alternate universe only understood by them; for the minute at least.

She stroked her stomach. It certainly did not look the same as it did just seven years ago. It used to be something to be envied; defined, taut and, most enviably, flat. Now it resembled one of those wobbling three-tiered jellies on a plate. For all she aimed to do something about this jiggling pile of skin every Monday, it just seemed to be Friday again before she knew it and the cold, crisp glass of New Zealand heaven was already being poured. Who knew there were so many calories in wine? And, more importantly, who knew you would see these calories accumulate magnificently around your hips and thighs after housing a small human, or four, for nine months? Oh, but that sound as the golden liquid sloshes at the bottom of a crystal glass, leaving the tears of wine around the inner rim made those love handles just a little bit worth it.

'I don't know how you do it,' Katherine remarked. She had been in the company of her childhood friend for the last half an hour; having a brew in the sunshine, chit-chatting about absolutely nothing and everything all at the same time. They were so good at that. It made it easy for her to grab a few moments of mind drifting while Katherine kept a watchful eye on the inmates.

She snapped out of her daydream. The once relatively calm game of fairies and gorillas had descended into utter chaos. The twins were now screaming, if you could describe the high-pitched wailing noise as a scream. Probably a cross between a howl and a squeal, a sqowl or a howeel; she let her mind blend the two words for a second. She used to be an English teacher before she decided to give it up after the twins' arrival. Juggling motherhood and a teaching job was just about manageable with two children. The addition of two more, at the same time, was just a bit much, even for her, the epitome of organisation. She thanked her lucky stars that she had Jonathan, her husband. He was always her champion and made her huge decision to put her career on hold, to be a full-time mom, an easy one.

No, now was not the time; back to reality and dealing with the situation. A fairy had been decapitated and justice needed to prevail.

Katherine slipped out of the side gate; she would most definitely not want to witness the parenting style about to take place; 'soft touch' as opposed to a military operation she liked to oversee. They were chalk and cheese in their approaches to just about everything; the dummy police to the pacifier advocate! Their friendship could be conceived as an odd pairing but it just worked; most of the time. They were definitely the Ying to each other's Yang!

It was actually quite funny how they had both turned out. As a child, Katherine was that laid back she was almost horizontal; absolutely nothing bothered her. Every play date as kids required wading across the sea of clothes, toys and used drinks cups to find a spot to play in. For her now to be the parent who despised fingerprints, cushions out of place and required every jigsaw piece to be counted back into the box was most definitely a turn up for the books. Katherine the adult was regimented and full of views on everything. Perhaps four children and a dog smooth out the sharp edges and black and white views. Katherine was a Prison Officer to the core and she was brilliant at doing it her way. Different did not equate to right or wrong.

But, move over Military Mama, she thought to herself, Soft Touch is working it today! She beamed at herself. Judge Mammy had managed to satisfy all; prosecution and defendants alike. Gorilla's owner was sentenced to digging the hole for the fairy to be laid to rest. Mud was flying everywhere, hand-trowels were no longer being used and the picking of flower heads to throw in the grave – the irony almost funny – was a go-go! She oversaw the beautifully arranged pots being ransacked – geraniums being plucked at, lobelias strewn all over the patio and the busy Lizzies being yanked at so they could never be busy again – and winced just a little. The entire debacle was ridiculously joyous, even if a little morbid. She was not about to explain life and death today, though, so she let them enjoy their moment. Peace and order had resumed. Nothing soft about this approach at all.

To the outsider looking in, she thought that her life may seem boring, for want of a better word. For her, there was nothing more rewarding than banishing gorillas to the outer side of space, creating fairy gardens and conquering moments of parenting that could have erupted into four crying children but instead evolved into moments of resolution and total pleasure.

She looked on in sheer amazement at the little humans she'd created, helped teach and grow.

Tonight, she would toast her little darlings and her super efforts of parenting. It was a Friday, at least.

★★★

Sarah Simpson nee Lake lives in Teesside with her husband and their four children. She is an ex-teacher turned online business owner and team coach. *Connections* is Sarah's first published work and she now can't wait to get stuck into her next writing project.
If you want to learn more about what Sarah does follow her on Instagram: www.instagram.com/still.sas

COMING HOME

Steven Smith

"We choose to go to the moon. We choose to go to the moon in this decade and do the other things, not because they are easy, but because they are hard, because that goal will serve to organize and measure the best of our energies and skills, because that challenge is one that we are willing to accept, one we are unwilling to postpone, and one which we intend to win, and the others, too."

That's what President John F. Kennedy told the nation back in September of 1962. A bold man with big ambitions. He had a vision. Back then, nobody would have dared dream so big. He did though, wanting to put us on the moon. Why did he want to do this? Because he wanted to see if it could be done. To push the envelope of human ingenuity and adventure.

Though he never saw it, he made it happen. Kennedy set about a race that enthralled the world and saw the best and brightest create the technology to safely make lunar exploration a reality. You see, that's the thing with human curiosity. Sometimes we have to do something just to see why. It's like that sign warning us 'Do Not Push' or 'Wet Paint' – sometimes we have to reach out and test it, we have to know. And just because we could, we went back to that little grey rock spinning around our home five more times. We kicked some rocks, scooped some dust, ran some tests to learn more. Just because we were curious.

And that curiosity spurred us on to even greater heights, even if the priorities shifted. NASA became enthralled by the planet that has spawned so many stories. That one red planet that we so often imagine being home to other intelligent life. Mars. Throughout the twenty-first century, many missions were launched to explore the dusty red surface in search of life, or the ability to sustain life.

The probes and rovers sent over the years succeeded. They found evidence of water below the surface. The atmosphere was less than ideal but that could be solved. And so, plans were formulated – how soon could we put people on Mars? It took more time than anyone imagined. The journey was long and would put a strain on the human body. We weren't meant to spend that long flying through space. Space agencies all raced to be the first to make the arduous journey. NASA started out using what they already knew – the moon was achievable.

Privately, they set about establishing a base from which further missions could be launched. The plan was to run trials, send rockets to Mars and study the data gathered from the journey. Within the decade, the hope was to send astronauts to the red planet. Things changed. Before testing had a chance to yield any meaningful data, something happened. An armada of rockets was launched to the moon. Each one carried additional crew, cargo, resources and the components designed for the spacecraft intended to convey us to Mars.

I'd been on the moon for three long years, spurred on by this curiosity. I'd not seen my family or friends for longer. But I got the chance to visit the moon, walk about its surface. Something so many people still hadn't had a chance to experience. My role was to take part in the exercises that would replicate the conditions for the journey to Mars. I was expecting to have returned to Earth long before the long-distance ship arrived. Whispered conversations spread through the colony and high-security messages passed to the higher ranks only served to increase the gossip. The situation on Earth had worsened. Between pandemics, viral warfare and climate change, humanity was tearing its home apart. Sending manned missions to Mars was no longer a curiosity, it became imperative.

The base, once placid, tranquil almost, was a hive of activity. The vast construction hangars were alive with the best and brightest minds working to assemble three vast vessels. The rockets and shuttles of the past were familiar. The Saturn Vs were something to behold – enormous constructions reaching for the heavens. And the power they generated to break gravity and carry on ever higher into the cold embrace of space was mindblowing. The shuttles were something else. Two sleek white reusable boosters to get the whole thing off the ground, a cumbersome orange-brown fuel tank to keep the shuttle supplied and the shuttle itself. They looked like an aircraft to some extent and were the first method of truly reusable space travel; these new vehicles were like nothing else. All sleek lines and shining chrome, they wouldn't look out of place in a sci-fi film. Having received my orders, watching them being assembled filled me with equal parts excitement and fear.

★

They had the gleaming vessels completed in just over a month. It was incredible to think something so technologically and mechanically advanced could be constructed so fast. It left me with a tinge of apprehension. It would only take one person to overlook one little screw or rivet, the tiniest component, to cause the complete destruction of the craft in the vacuum of space. But time was not on our side. The crew prepared for an early start with final health checks and a one-night stay in an isolated suite. Sparse though they were, they ensured limited exposure to anything prior to launch. Everything occurred in a blur of frenetic activity as final preparations were made and the launch procedure began. Strapped into uncomfortable seats in only slightly more comfortable spacesuits, the doors were locked and sealed. The next time they opened, they would reveal the red dust of the Martian surface.

Our time preoccupied with pre-launch checks, ensuring engines, fuel lines and systems were all fully primed and showing no indications of faults, the countdown began. The cramped cabin aside, the spacecraft felt decidedly different to the rockets that conveyed me to the Moon. For one thing, they carried forty men and women each. Though there was no escaping the vibrations of the engines powering up, they felt far less violent than those on a rocket. It was a strange feeling, looking out of the vast glass frontage at the empty blackness of space. On the monitors, the moon grew smaller, the green and blue view of Earth receding rapidly with it. Thirty years ago, back when a global pandemic swept the planet in 2020, the journey would have taken the better part of seven months. Between the pandemic and other global issues, accelerated technological advancements cut the journey to three months. An impressive feat no doubt, but it would still be a long journey. Plenty long enough for us to worry over what we may find on Mars.

★

The journey was uneventful to the point of being boring. The landing was less straightforward. None of our data had ever indicated that Mars suffered atmospheric storms. Electrical strikes knocked out navigation systems. With zero visibility, all three vessels got separated, and atmospheric interference meant the comms systems were useless. The landing was rough, the ship damaged due to the rugged landscape. I still had a job to do. Though many of the crew remained aboard to make repairs to the vessel and attempt contact with the other teams, a small group headed out into the barren landscape.

I felt a deep sense of unease. The surface was arid and rocky. Dust everywhere. How the planet would sustain life, I could not fathom. But that was not my concern. The scientists deemed it to be the best chance for humanity, had run all the data, analysed all the samples. They must know what they were talking about. Our small party stepped out from the weak shadow of the damaged craft, testing the reduced gravity. It was a strange sensation. It was stronger, more present than on the moon, but not nearly as strong as Earth. It would take some adjusting to after so long on the moon. Syncing our devices to the tracking beacon of the ship, we all headed out in different directions, aiming to cover more ground. Some were looking for the ideal place to start a settlement, others sought resources. I fell into the latter bracket. I had a hunch that if there was any water to be found, it wouldn't be on the surface.

An hour-long hike brought me to a vast cliff face stretching up into the swirling maelstrom of dust. A large cavern mouth opened up at its base. No light seemed to reach more than ten feet inside. The large LED lamps mounted to my helmet helped push back the shadows. The roaring of the wind outside dulled to a low howl, getting quieter the deeper I walked. More than once I paused, certain I had heard a noise. A chittering, scrabbling sound just on the edge of my hearing. It made my blood run cold. Every time I looked at where the noises seemed to come from, I found nothing. As I descended, the frigid temperatures of the surface slowly rose. Soon I could swear the sound of dripping water reached me. The narrow tunnels opened into a vast cavern with an enormous lake of water. It was sludgy brown, thick and unappealing. As its surface rippled, it appeared almost alive such was its thickness. Testing it with my scanner, my concerns were confirmed. Completely unsuitable. Its toxicity was too high to salvage for any human use, and even showed alarming levels of radioactivity.

That wasn't good. I had hoped, expected to find one of two things. Nothing at all, or a semi-fresh source of water that we could work with. What I had found was the worst possible outcome. It made no sense. There were no known chemicals or minerals on Mars that could cause this.

Around the lake was another tunnel stretching further down beneath the Martian surface. Something caught my eye as I rounded the corner that made my blood run cold. Bones. From what, I had no idea. But it was very clearly a pile of bones. My hand rested on the butt of the gun at my hip. I had no idea whether it would work here on Mars. And even if it did, who knew what I might be using it against.

I moved on hastily, not wanting to look too closely at the remains. Every little noise now sent me into a panic. Was I being watched? Followed? None of this was expected, it didn't fit with the reports we were given. I tripped and stumbled away from the macabre mound of bones, deeper into the tunnel. The further I went, the less natural the tunnel seemed to be. It looked like it had been carved out of the rock. Further in, the floor was littered with unusual-looking tools, containers and chemical barrels. All very-much manufactured. Something really wasn't right.

The tunnel opened out into a small square room. It contained rows of desks covered in thick red dust. Each was set up with a range of equipment. It looked like some kind of computer hardware. Nothing like what was seen on Earth. This looked far more advanced. A low humming sound filled the room. They were still running. One machine, in the far corner of the room, emitted a fuzzy glow. Curiosity got the better of me. I strode over, standing in front of the weathered desk. A small, thin disc-shaped object was the source of the glow. Swiping at it with a gloved hand cleared dust from its surface, the hazy image instantly sharpening. A glowing holographic representation of a globe. Of the Earth. It spun lazily in the dusty air. A series of figures fluctuated in a box floating above the planetary depiction. They highlighted the population, ever decreasing as had been the case for decades. They also showed the remaining amount of minerals and resources on the planet. All dwindling far faster than most people had any idea about.

This was worrying. Who or what was observing Earth? Possibly more troubling than this was why they were watching. A noise from a passage behind drew my full attention. Drawing my weapon, I cautiously headed down the sterile metal tunnel. Open doors revealed what seemed like living quarters running down its length. Halfway down the passage, an open door spilt a pale light. Inside, a small desk and lamp sat against the back wall. It was littered with documents and scraps of paper. All typed in English. The date on them was bizarre, entirely alien to me. It outlined the destruction of Mars. War. Famine. Plague. Overpopulation. Pollution. Dwindling resources. Atmospheric change.

I shivered. It read like the recent history of Earth.

If I didn't know what I was reading, I'd have easily believed it was the rationale put together to leave Earth. A planet-wide population that had grown, evolved and expanded physiologically and technologically, over time their needs drove them to strip the planet of all viable resources and poison it with its waste. A once-beautiful place now barren and dry. Wealth and greed drove those with means to horde what they could. Friction became tension. Tension led to scuffles. Scuffles became a global war. Factions, nations, turned against one another. One group launched attacks against another to take what they had for their own. The parallels with what was happening on Earth was horrifying.

A plan was set in motion, outlined in clinical detail in the document. To relocate and repopulate their civilisation elsewhere, on a nearby planet. Their plight mirrored our own perfectly. A scrawled note on the final page caught my eye. My hope rapidly turned to dread as I read it. 'CAELUM ORBIS: OUR LAST HOPE'. The people of Mars had fled to Earth. We had fled to Earth. The knowledge had somehow been lost, and now we vainly hoped to migrate back to where we started. Humanity had not evolved on Earth. He had come from here, Mars, and colonised Earth as our own. And now it seemed we were set to repeat the mistakes of our past.

A shuffling noise at the door, along with a wheezing, heralded the unseen arrival of a humanoid figure, shadowed in the gloom. With a rasping voice, he uttered a short phrase.

"You should not have returned here. Humanity has

failed. None shall survive." A sharp pain exploded through my skull before everything went black.

★★★

Steven has been an avid reader for as long as he can remember. In school, he loved writing stories. In 2015, he set up a blog to review his then-reading obsession – the Discworld series. Over time the reviews branched out and he added new reading-based features.

In late 2019, an idea for a story struck, so he took part in NaNoWriMo to keep him honest. Throughout 2020 that idea eventually became his first novel, *Chasing Shadows*. In late 2020 he had finally finished revising it, ready for editing and release in early 2021.
He's also been hard at work on his second novel, the follow up to *Chasing Shadows* and trying his hand at a whole host of short stories to boot.

https://authorstevensmith.co.uk/
https://www.amazon.co.uk/Steven-Smith/e/
B08Z8JXLYD?ref_=dbs_p_ebk_r00_abau_000000
https://www.goodreads.com/author/show/21297044.
Steven_Smith

TRANS-SIBERIAN SITUATION

Zoe Brooks

She woke as the carriage shook and rattled over a bump. Her cabin mates stirred but no one spoke. She immediately knew that she felt dreadful. She had a splitting headache from dehydration, and she was extremely hungry. Was it too early for noodles? Her water bottle had fallen from her high bunk, onto the floor of the cabin. She was going to have to get up and retrieve it. She climbed down carefully, noting the position of Emma's head near the ladder, so that she didn't step on it. She also noted, smiling, that Brian had snuck into the bunk with Emma. It was a tight squeeze, but they looked peaceful. Once she had got down safely, she set about finding her lost water, her shoes, some wet wipes and a mug, all without disturbing the others. She quietly slid the door to the corridor open and headed to the loo at the end of the carriage. She could feel the vodka seeping out of her pores, the air in the carriage still heavy with the smell of stale cigarette smoke, and it turned her stomach. She opened one of the windows to let some fresh air flow through the carriage. Thankfully there was no one else around. She checked her watch, but it was on Moscow time; she certainly didn't have the brain capacity to work out the time difference, but it must have been early.

The loo was not in a good state, it had been heavily frequented by the occupants of the entire carriage during the previous night's events and, evidently, the more vodka that went down, the messier things got. What had started out as chatting with the cabin next door had snowballed until the entire carriage was drinking, smoking and sharing snacks whilst trying to converse in broken English, German and French, followed by a quick-fire lesson in Russian swear words, then a finale of songs in various languages. She tried to focus on the track visible through the hole in the squat toilet, rushing past below, and the fresh icy air streaming through the window, but it was no good. She retched uncontrollably, the kind where you can barely stand. There was nothing in her body to bring back, she just had to wait for it to pass.

Shivering, she did her best to regain composure and wash in the cold water sink with the wet wipes available. Luckily, she had thought ahead and braided her hair tight to her head before leaving Moscow three days ago, so she just had to smooth down the frizzy bits. They were only halfway through their train journey and she was already questioning her sanity in agreeing to this trip.

Feeling slightly better, she emerged from the loo, coating her hands thoroughly with alcohol gel. She filled her mug at the samovar (large constantly boiling hot water urn) and tipped in the pre-mixed coffee, milk powder and sugar sachet; it was no Starbucks, but it would do. She stood by the open window and took careful sips. Dimitri came out of his cabin looking surprisingly fresh, already with his first cigarette of the day in his mouth. He nodded with an almost undetectable smile and shook his cigarettes at her. 'No thank you,' she shuddered, almost retching again. She could not imagine a cigarette right now. He shrugged and walked past her to the gap in between the carriages, which had been designated the 'unofficial smoking area'.

She watched the monotonous grey scenery flying by, literally just vast expanses of forest, no houses, no animals or people. For the first day or so she had been fascinated, but train life was starting to get a little bit stale, not to mention confusing. There was an approximate list of stops and the duration on a plastic card on the wall in Cyrillic (all in Moscow time, which could be anything from five hours different to the local time, if you knew what the local time was, if you knew where you were...). She had been using this card along with her guidebook to try and guess which stops were which and how long each would be. So far, they had been quite accurate, but none of the group had dared venture too far from the train, just in case it had started moving and left them stranded in Siberia. This was how they had ended up chatting to Dimitri and his brother Sacha in the neighbouring cabin; Brian had been insistent that the stop the previous day was at least thirty minutes and went to find a vendor selling ANYTHING other than noodles, but he had literally jumped back onto the train with seconds to spare waving something made of bread. After that, Dimitri had tried to help decipher the stops for the remaining time onboard the train. He had also taken them to the restaurant cart and translated the menu. All of the guidebooks had suggested packet food like soup and noodles, which required only boiling water from the samovar, as that was the only thing guaranteed to be constantly available on the train.

Luckily for them, Dimitri's English was excellent, from what she could understand and remember from his story the previous evening (which was hazy). He and his brother were travelling home to Irkutsk to visit their mother. Dimitri had a lot of questions: 'But you are guide? You are not speaking the language, how is this possible?' She had tried to explain that she was standing in for the usual guide, but she also didn't want to say too much in front of the clients. She basically worked in the office of a tour operator in the UK, she had done the tour (St Petersburg to Beijing) before and got shipped in due to the usual guide being unavailable. The plan was that she chaperoned the group on the trains between the cities and they used local guides in each destination. All she had to do was make sure the group were happy (well, that's how her boss sold it to her). She had been given a set of notes to follow; admittedly, the five-day train journey between Moscow and Irkutsk had not been on her list of disadvantages whilst weighing up the pros and cons of a month off work travelling.

Dimitri had emerged from the smoking area. 'You will not see anything different out there, all the same.' He gestured to the window. He pointed to the card listing the stops, which made no sense. 'Today we will stop for one hour at 13:00 Moscow time in Omsk, tell your group, they might be able to pay for a shower, your friend Brian, maybe he can get some more food!' She wanted to laugh at the way he said it but she knew he was serious, there was no attempt at humour. 'My brother, Sacha, he will watch your bags if you need him to.' She nodded and said thank you to Dimitri. She had been very lucky in that the group were incredibly laid back and well travelled, so they didn't appear to mind that she couldn't understand the damn card or communicate on their behalf.

She decided to finish her coffee back in her bunk and try her phone. Her reception had been intermittent, and she needed to reconfirm their arrival time with the local operator in Irkutsk. A message popped up, it was her boyfriend, Chris. He was checking on her, and he was missing her; she smiled, she missed him terribly. They hadn't been together that long, but they had been friends for years, and they worked together. She wished he could have joined them, he'd be loving it and would definitely get along with Brian. Their relationship had actually come about as the result of an affair. She had left her partner of six years for Chris. She was still dealing with pangs of guilt from her actions, and judgemental comments from mutual 'friends'. In her defence, they had been living almost separate lives, more like housemates, as their chosen careers took them on separate paths. She was sure that in an ideal world you worked at it, had date nights and weekends away, but not where Ian was concerned. She had drifted and he had let her, without so much as a shrug. Chris, it turns out, had always had his eye on her, but settled for being friends. They were currently in their first six months of living together.

Upon entering the cabin, she was returned to their reality, assessing the devastation from the previous night – at least two bottles of vodka had been sunk. Various empty mixer bottles and snacks lay strewn across the floor of the four-berth cabin. Emma was sitting up and dressed, attempting to tidy up but sighing quite a lot. 'It would help if I could bend down without my head hurting!' She did look quite pale. Brian was sitting cheerfully chomping on wasabi peas and rubbing his sinus area when he got a hot one. Drew was apparently able to communicate but had to stay lying down and keep his eyes closed. She tried the next cabin, where the other two clients, sisters Jackie and Lynette, were chatting and laughing. They were feeling fine and had apparently found the dining cart with Dimitri's help, but they couldn't quite recall what they ate!

Her phone beeped; this time it wasn't Chris. It was Alexei, the operator in Irkutsk confirming the itinerary and pick-up time at the train station for the transfer to Listvyanka, a small village on the shores of Lake Baikal.

The remaining two days were spent on the train, happily drinking vodka, although slightly more carefully, playing cards, eating whatever snacks they could get from the stops, sharing said snacks and generally getting to know the other carriage occupants. The worn fixtures and fittings, frayed carpets, greasy door handles and attempts to appease the bad-tempered cleaning ladies all became entirely normal and actually quite fun. The constant movement and the need to grab onto things for balance at any given time became an instant reaction. She could now see why people chose this trip.

At around midday on day five, the group finally left the train, backpacks on, unwashed and blinking into the sunlight as they stepped down onto the platform in Irkutsk. The group said their goodbyes to Dimitri and Sacha and thanked them for all their help. Lynette, in particular, had taken a shine to Dimitri and had planned to meet up with him again before the group left for Mongolia.

She scanned the waiting crowd for some sort of sign of their pickup. A large bear of a man was waiting with a sign that appeared to say her name. As the only tourists on the train, they stuck out for miles, so the large man was soon by their side introducing himself as Alexei. He gestured for the group to follow him and led them to a large transit van. It would take up to an hour to get to Listvyanka and he was estimating that the visit with the shaman could take up a further hour. 'I can see that most of the group are Australians, they usually need to eat every two hours in the cold, or they cease to function. I have supplies in the van and I will ring ahead to the guest house and organise dinner for our arrival.' Again, she scanned his face for some attempt at humour, but nothing. She would never get used to Russians!

After the group returned and squidged themselves into the van, he introduced himself and explained the itinerary and the options; he was clearly a very experienced guide and she was relieved to take a back seat for a few days.

Alexei talked as he drove about the style of houses, the culture, industry and his memories of growing up in the area. They eventually pulled up at the residence of the shaman. Alexei had managed the expectations of the group wonderfully and everyone knew how to behave and what to do. The shaman would not 'perform' on demand but he was happy to speak to the group. Alexei would translate as he saw fit for everyone. The group were led around the back of a 'normal looking' residence where they entered what appeared to be a yurt with a wood burning stove, which opened out into an outside space decorated with pieces of fabric. With Alexei translating, he explained the types of shaman and their tools, and how he came to realise his talents as a boy. He showed the group the music he liked to work with and where he liked to perform rituals. He also explained some simple rituals and the kind of work he did within his community. He then went on to explain how spirits can enter a shaman. The group asked questions and Alexei continued to translate in both directions. As the group were leaving, they left offerings and said their thank yous and goodbyes. Brian was already plotting how he could induce some sort of shamanic trance for himself.

After the evening meal, Alexei asked her to join him in the garden of the large wooden guest house. 'It is always good to plan the day ahead without the clients.' He certainly loved a plan! 'Tonight, I will not stay in the guest house as I live with my wife in the village; this is better for me. I also need to give you some information. This is awkward for me, but I must be truthful. As we were leaving the shaman, he was very grateful and shaking my hand a lot, saying he was excited that there is a new life within the group. I am at first thinking of my wife, but this is not possible, but the shaman tells me it is you. I think he is saying you are pregnant? No?' She was tired and struggling to follow what Alexei was saying. He continued regardless, 'I know that in the west you like to do the test and I don't even know if you have the husband or boyfriend? So, my apologies if this is not appropriate, but this is something you should know. Here, the family will go to the shaman more than the drug store.'

She sat processing, frowning and finally wincing with embarrassment, shaking her head. It was ridiculous! How did a man who had simply looked at her and sat in the same room know this? How was this even remotely possible? She sat on the wooden bench, feeling like the world was spinning without her, unsure of how to respond. Was it definitely meant for her? Why her? Could it not have been the other girls in the group?

Alexei interrupted her thoughts, already planning ahead. 'If you prefer, I can send my wife to the drug store with you tomorrow. I can take the group on an orientation walk and give them ideas of what to do here? Maybe this will help, and you get the test. My wife's English is also very good. I will let you decide, we have time here, it is no problem. But you need to know if the shaman is right, no?'

She nodded, not necessarily in agreement, but to make him shut up. He took the hint and went to join the group inside the house. It was absolutely absurd, but she decided that the best course of action would be to shrug it off for now and do some sort of humiliating test in the morning, to please everyone else and put the whole thing behind her. Despite her immediate reservations, she certainly didn't want to disrespect anyone's beliefs in the shaman. She sat for a little while in the garden of the guest house, looking at the spectacular scenery, the twinkling lights of the village and the moon's reflection glistening on Lake Baikal. She went back into the dining room, where some of the group were chatting. Brian and Drew were comparing theories on how you could potentially make your own vodka, looking at ingredients and techniques. She joined in and did her best to forget about it.

The next morning, Alexei's wife, Irina, was almost as she imagined, a carbon copy of Elsa, from *Frozen*. The walk to the shops was awkward to say the least, especially as Irina and Alexei had been longing for a child of their own for some time, and here she was like some sort of badly behaved teenager, unplanned and caught out by the village shaman. After Irina and the lady behind the counter having a seemingly rather shouty chat about her in Russian, she was handed a bag and she was very pleased to escape back to the guest house. She sat for a while looking at the instructions, and also checked the brand on the internet. Enough stalling... She sat and waited for the time stated and then looked at the bit of plastic. There was a definite line, and paler line next to it, which was that? She checked the internet again, in case the instructions weren't to be trusted. It was positive. She swore quietly.

She sat watching the tap dripping. So now what? Did she tell Chris, but then not see him for another two weeks? Leave him worrying whilst she travelled through Mongolia and China...

Maybe she wouldn't tell him at all for now... Could

it be a false positive? Things with Chris were going so well, but they hadn't really discussed this sort of thing. What if she lost it whilst travelling anyway? Was 'it' the wrong thing to call it…? She laughed out loud at her own ignorance. Didn't you get morning sickness, when did that start? How was she going to cover that up? How far along was she anyway?! She swore again, a few more times, then laughed wondering if it had ears yet, then cried. She really was delighted if more than a little shocked. Now all she had to do was look after it.

★★★

Zoe Brooks currently lives in Leicestershire with her family. After seven years in London, working for an adventure travel tour operator, her writing is mainly focused on her many travel experiences. She now works as a Virtual Assistant, specialising in social media, online content creation, travel planning and business development services. She also coordinates her local child friendly business networking group.

SIGNE A DIVINE VIKING WARRIOR

Kelly Vikings

An intense pain was felt throughout her entire body, unlike anything she had ever experienced before. Although unable to move, she tried desperately to break free. Her hands and feet were tied. Her long, silver, knotted hair falling across her face, hiding her moment of terror as they continued to watch.

In the distance, she sensed him in the crowds. His deep brown eyes watching her. He too was motionless, hands tied, being forced back by fighters.

A rag bound her mouth; she was unable to communicate. She desperately wanted to shout to him, her forbidden love, for he was always the only one, her only love; there had never been anyone else in her entire existence in this realm.

The burning sensation was racing towards her toes, she was struggling to see through the smoke. The fire engulfed her as she hung tied, unable to break free. She was stronger than life itself and never showed weakness in battle; she was not scared of death, of entering Valhalla. She would sacrifice her soul to the gods, especially to the goddess Freyja, as her sisters and mothers had done before her.

The smell of her skin, beginning to burn. Tears welling in her eyes as she lifted her head to see children watching her in the distance. Their mothers and fathers holding them tight. Signe spotted a girl and her mother, whom she had helped to heal from sickness just a few moons ago, watching with despair as the flames began to rise.

This was a sacred Viking settlement, it was 1021. Signe was being burnt alive for acts of witchery that her queen had set a trial for and, as a result, the villagers had sentenced her to death. In today's world, the witchery that she was accused of would be acceptable, yet before, in a time when such things were unexplained, it was her fate and destiny to set her soul free to be reborn again. Aware of her previous four lifetimes, she knew exactly what was going to happen to her. Having spent three sunrises tied naked to a tree, she'd experienced men raping her, farmers and their children throwing rotten berries and faeces at her and she had not eaten for many days.

In many ways she was grateful this was the end. The only things that had kept her in this settlement were the deep brown eyes she was seeing for what she thought was the last time.

★

Njal's father was a king; he had never experienced love from him. Kings in the Viking world were ruled by Thor.

He had no time for anything other than whores and battles. Njal was tired, he had spent this last summer harvesting, fishing, helping to govern his people, their lands, protecting their settlements from rogue traders and Viking fighters. He had earnt the respect of his village and people, he had protected them, kept them safe, fed them and drunk mead with them, given them hope of greener new lands and far away treasures.

His father, who had sailed last summer, was yet to return. Njal was unsure if he was ever going to see his father again, but he always thought he would set sail after the harsh winter months, cross the shores, to discover exactly what had happened to him. His mum, their queen, was a Viking queen, she had the respect of all the shield maidens. Her fiercely driven and protective nature captured the hearts of everyone in their village. Yet, she was lonely and had found comfort in the arms of another woman. Njal had discovered this and had tried to keep this hidden from his people.

Njal had first fallen into the arms of Signe during a battle in a neighbouring village. She had the spirit of a real queen, she led with love, was beautiful, unbreakable and fearless. Her eyes were petrifyingly blue, silver hair fell to her wildfire. Every time he thought of her naked, her perfectly shaped breasts, he became aroused, and yet it was always a dream, the touch of her silky skin; he often wondered what was to be discovered under her clothes.

He could not believe she was a healer. She was a witch and his god had presented her as a gift to him. The villagers had tried to uncover her witchery, to bring her to trial. His mother had instructed the village guards to tie her to an oak tree to bring her to communal trial. He believed his queen, his own mother, was jealous. He had seen how she watched Signe; he was to marry a king's daughter, not a mere shield maiden, and definitely not a witch.

The gods had decided now was her time, the moon had declared it as it glowed in the night's sky, the sea reflecting its beauty. Earlier, when they found Signe guilty, they started the ceremony and her sacrifice by drinking goat's blood. Njal's mother had made Signe walk, still unclothed, down to the wooden firepit.

The stars in the skies were much brighter than ever before, the moon shone on the guilty, as they took his one true love. Njal vowed he would never bare his soul to anyone until the gods entwined them together in a new life.

He watched, desperately trying to break free to save her. He could see them light the bottom of the firepit laid below her toes. Her naked body, brutally bruised, scars cutting deep across her back, he knew she was helpless, unable to do anything, he could hear the fire burn and then…

A silver and blue spark lit up the entire sky. The moon glowed brighter than ever before. It was an incredible moment; unlike anything he'd ever seen before. The sea glowed and he saw it… a man walked out of the sea, between other women, swimming around him. He was far bigger, stronger than any other man he had fought before, he was a god. This god walked through to Signe, but before he could do anything, Njal realised the guards had shielded him and his vision. He felt fabric cover his head, now he could only hear... Njal heard the crowds, noises of panic and horror, he could hear horses gallop, swords, arrows and fighting, children screaming. There was utter chaos. He could even smell the sweat and blood. This had to be an act from the gods.

Njal felt himself being pushed. Hands removed the fabric from his head. It was at this moment, he caught a glimpse of a white stallion galloping past him, with the outline of Signe straddled over its back. He knew it was her, she must be alive, he had to rescue her.

Njal's instinct was to hunt down his gold, iron sword, armoury and horse and flee to save Signe. The sounds of the horse's hooves were now distant, he was sure she would be followed, his mother would make sure of it. He had to protect Signe.

In that moment, he felt a hand on his shoulder. It was his mother, her arm resting on his shoulder as she asked him for his forgiveness. Her guards untied him, stood down and gave him space to see and breathe again. His mother ordered them to go and protect the village. She begged for Njal's forgiveness again, her only son.

Njal knew every inch of his body wanted to murder his mother. She had been untrue, unfaithful, jealous and her governance of the settlement and its warriors was not what his god, Thor, saw as being truthful. He glanced at her in disgust, turned to walk towards where Signe's body had been set alight, then walked towards the sea's edge, where the incredibly strong man, a Viking god, had mysteriously appeared and set Signe free. However, he had now miraculously disappeared.

Njal knew what he must do. He had gold, weapons, horses; he must claim them, then follow Signe's tracks to be reunited. He would be leaving everything he had experienced since he was a young boy and old enough to remember. His father would never forgive him, but he had to follow the desire of his heart, or he would rather take his life and enter Valhalla.

Njal turned to his mother, who was on her knees begging for his forgiveness. He saw her lover beside her. He went to her, his queen. Taking her hand, he slyly took her knife and turned; within seconds, Njal had cut deep into the throat of her lover, and then turned and fled. He didn't look back; he heard his mother's screams. He wanted her to feel the pain he had experienced, and he knew she would. That was his parting gift; he would never forgive her for what she had done, and he knew he would never return.

★

The morning always made Signe happiest. The woods were where she enjoyed foraging for plants and wild mushrooms. She loved the mud as she often walked barefoot and loved listening to the birds. As she lay there still unclothed, she felt her body feel discomfort, as the morning sun began to warm her. She opened her eyes and gasped, as she realised partly what had happened the night before. Looking down to her toes, she felt extreme pain.

Why was she breathing in this age? Her eyes were still stinging from the smoke, she saw a stream below her and tried to untie the ropes that were tying her feet and hands loosely. As she did so, she heard a branch crack. Spinning around, unknowing of where she was, or how she had got there, she saw the most beautiful white stallion, as he fed himself on the grass close by.

Signe saw some bags wrapped over the gentle stallion. She knew she had to break free and wash herself first. There was still the smell of blood and smoke on her skin, in her hair. She knew her feet were sore, burnt, but looking down she knew she would be okay. She was extremely lucky to be alive. As she set her wrists and then her feet free, Signe bathed in the stream, washing her silvery hair, bathing her eyes. She shared a blessing to the gods, to thank Freyja for her love and protection.

Signe walked across to the most beautiful stallion she had ever seen. She stroked his neck and nuzzled his face. He was strong and loyal, she knew it. She took the bags off him and looked inside, discovering food, leather trousers, a cloak made of hawk feathers and even some gold. A piece of treasure, a golden pin with a symbol of a tree. An oak tree, maybe the Yggdrasil – world tree – a scared tree that her ancestors before her would have prayed to. She sensed this meant something to her future self.

Signe lit a fire and dressed herself with the cloak and trousers for warmth. It took several sunrises to heal, and she enjoyed the power of pause. At night, the moon had gifted her bright skies, sleeping close to her only companion, her stallion, as she lay close to him for warmth.

On the fourth rise, she decided to make a new shield. She carved this from an oak that she felt drawn to. Having found some tools in one of the bags, she made a wooden sword, but knew this was not enough to protect her from steel swords or arrows. Signe healed her wounds and bruises having created potions from the Earth's soul. She felt herself strengthening. On the eighth rise, she felt ready to ride. She hid any signs of where she had rested and then left, riding along a path, keeping hidden through the twists and turns of the old oaks, where she believed spirits existed and were protecting her.

★

Njal grabbed all he could, before fleeing the settlement. He had no idea if, or where he would be reunited with his one true love Signe. He had ridden for what felt like an eternity and he knew riding alone was an increased risk. At night he would look up at the stars, wondering if Signe was doing the same as him, wishing for her safety and protection. He would never go back to his birth settlement or forgive his mother for what she had so cruelly done to him.

It had been almost a full moon since he had left. Njal was beginning to lose hope of ever finding Signe again. He came upon a small settlement of shield maidens. He was invited to stay, given food, refuge and comfort. That evening one of the shield maidens with beautiful golden hair came to him naked and asked him to sleep with her. He kissed her lips, hungering for Signe, and touched her youthful skin. He placed his hand between her warmth and felt himself grow, but he stopped and pushed her away. The girl cried, knelt on her knees begging for his love, she was only a young girl. He explained he had a love; he was waiting for her. He would never love another like he loved Signe.

The young girl lay next to him that night and as they woke up to a new day. He helped the shield maidens to rebuild a roof with timber that was far too heavy for them to lift, providing them extra safety, as he prepared to say goodbye at sunrise. The women Viking warriors lit a fire, and Njal flinched; the smell of fire was making him feel sick. They talked all through the night with the moon above them, sharing stories of their gods and singing until the early sunrise. He talked about Signe and the sea god who saved her from the fire sent by his mother.

The women directed Njal to leave on a path leading to a settlement they had spoken well of, where he could find refuge, buy armoury, fighters, and he could ask for any sightings of Signe.

*

Signe had been riding for many sunrises. She was tired of the woodlands and wanted to find some company. There was a path she knew she would connect to, where there was a sacred village of shield maidens; she knew she would be safe there. Looking up to the stars, she wondered about her one true love, asking herself, the universe, if she would ever see him again. Njal was the only man to ever hold her heart.

Signe spent days making arrows, shields and potions, casting spells, often to the moon gods and the goddess

Freyja. She questioned why she was still here and what her purpose was. Why had her life been spared? She rode along a winding path, along the clifftops, which led her to a place where she looked over a bay. She could see the sea, the sparkling of lights from very distant villages and for a moment she said a prayer, thanking the gods for her life, knowing how precious it truly was.

As she continued, there was a noise. She looked to see what it was, saw rabbits and grabbed her bow and arrows. Her favourite, a meal of rabbit; she stopped under a large oak and set up a fire. This was her first taste of meat in months. She felt happy as she enjoyed the stars, the warmth in her belly, and looked up to the skies. She knew this was a good sign, it had to be.

The next day she rode fast. She loved feeling the air through her hair, she felt free and alive. Seated on the most majestic horse she had ever been gifted, his sweat and hers, together they galloped across the lands. As she arrived at an opening, she saw a little village, the safety of the shield maidens. They saw her coming; in fact, one of the warriors said she had known of her coming. Giving Signe food and protection, in return she helped to heal two of the older shield maidens' wounds and helped a young mother with child who was in great discomfort to feel more comfortable. As they talked around the fire, the young lady who had laid by Njal's side stood with courage and asked if she was the Signe that knew Njal.

Signe was informed of his stay, of what had happened and where he was headed. The young girl asked if she could leave to offer her life to Signe as a protector and shield. Then two more asked their council for safe passage to leave to join Signe in her quest to tell fate-led prophecies and heal. As Signe left with her stallion, with new clothes gifted by these incredible ladies, she set a band of protection around the village and vowed to return again. Leaving together, they set off with one mission: to find Signe's true love, Njal.

Two moons had passed, and they were almost at the next village. Cautious of being discovered, Signe had covered her hair with a blanket. They rode onwards through the night. As the sun rose, they saw an eagle soaring over them. Ama, one of the shield maidens that rode with Signe, was gifted her name, eagle blood ran through her lifeline. She saw it follow them and as they reached the village it flew down. Ama reached out her arm for it to rest upon her. Signe passed Ama some rabbit to feed to the bird and, as it ate from her hand, she asked for it to send a message to Njal. Signe took her pin with the world tree and asked the bird to deliver it to Njal.

They entered the village with great caution. Vikings were welcoming, but if you said or did anything wrong, they were brutal, bloodthirsty and fearless. The women warriors entered with heightened senses. They saw children playing, heard wood carvers and iron welders make weapons and, dismounting their horses, they walked towards the longhouse.

As they tied up their horses, a farmer with his family stopped them, asking where they were from, why they were here. Estrid explained they were shield maidens and here to drink mead, find comfort and food. He seemed settled and, just as he was walking away, he turned to Signe and asked how she had such a fine horse. She answered with a warm smile and said her lover had gifted it to her, Njal. He looked at her with knowing then turned to walk away.

They spent two nights in the settlement, it was magnificent. A world away from where Signe had been; it is funny what you find worth in when you lose everything. Yet she was restless. Her heart ached; she desired her love.

In the midst of the night, she couldn't sleep. She grabbed her hawk feathered cloak and took herself off. The moon was full, and she could see very clearly. She was drawn towards the sea and walked along the wooden moorings. Signe was recalling what had happened to her, the days being left to brutal attacks from all those she had cared for, how she had been tied and torched. Still unclear on how she had been set free, how she had woken up by the lake, escaped, she wondered where Njal was. She knew he was alive, and she felt his presence close. She trusted in the divine gods that always guided her. It felt rather eery, and she knew she shouldn't stray far, but she felt like something was calling her. As she stepped to peer over the edge, her reflection was crystal clear.

She looked up to the moon and spoke a gentle ritual, one of releasing all that was, and accepting her fate. For a few seconds, she even considered a future without Njal. Her heart ached and she realised she was crying. Wiping her eyes, she noticed a small knörr; she could hear the oars gently paddling against the tide. Signe felt she should head back, but she was mesmerised by its gentle movement and intrigued to see who was sailing into the settlement at this time of night.

She waited until it was close to the side of the wooden mooring and started to hurry along the path back to her shield maidens. As she turned, she heard a voice. It couldn't be… she turned and knew immediately it was.

How could this be Njal, was she dreaming? He threw the anchor into the sea, leaped over the knörr onto the wooden mooring, and they both stared, running towards each other. She could see the depths of his brown eyes, as he could see the silveriness of her long hair in the moonlight. They ran towards each other and held each other tightly. He gently rested his head against her shoulder and whispered, "I will never let you go, never out of my sight, ever."

He picked Signe up into his arms and held her, carrying her to a wooden hut. A small holding. Njal had longed for Signe for too long, he had to take her. He threw her onto the wooden bed, removing his jacket and, in doing so, Signe recognised the world tree pin in his pocket; it almost glowed. She asked him where he had found this, and he replied an eagle had swooped down and dropped it to him. He explained he had taken a journey on his own, sailing to sell gold, but he knew this was a sign, he was being called to head back immediately to the settlement where he had been working for a farmer.

Signe knew this was the older man that had approached her, as they first arrived at the settlement. It all made sense now. She would tell Njal it was her who sent the message with the eagle, but for now she wanted to touch his skin, see his body naked, as the moon illuminated his muscles and she was wildly dancing inside with joy as he jumped onto the bed beside her.

They kissed gently at first, then he took his lips along the full outline of her body. She gently ran her fingers down his chest, through his hair, her head resting here for a few moments as she felt loved, safe and protected.

He felt for her, touching her, letting out a groan, eager to spin her around and take her, but Signe wanted to kiss his lips and feel him press his body against her. He looked into her beautiful eyes. Her hair was glowing, he touched her skin and they held each other close. He really wanted her, vowing nothing would ever divide them again, wishing they could stay in this moment for eternity. He had longed for this moment for so long; she was now his.

Waking up in each other's arms didn't feel real. After three full moons, Signe realised she was with child. They returned to the settlement of shield maidens. As they entered the quietness of the village, they saw a burial, life celebration taking place. It was the older shield maiden; her time had passed. They set her off in a Viking burial and watched her body burn as it floated out to sea. Signe and Njal knew they must stay, have their child here and protect the others, realising more than ever that what they had each seen as their endings was now only just the beginning...

Was this the start of a new world, the end of an age, an awakening? They vowed to lead with love, protect their sacred settlement every day, praying to the gods.

Njal never took his eyes far from Signe until her last peaceful breath, he her king, she his queen, never divided.

★★★

Kelly Vikings is a heart-led Business Leader, with a 'kick ass' warrior spirit. She mentors high profile, driven and energetically aligned women in business.
She works intuitively with Divine Feminine Energy, Numeric & Lunar Energy, mentoring female business leaders to align both their internal and external worlds, building strong business foundations to create success and divine wealth, in a guided, nurtured and impactful way.
No more hiding, it's your time to shine!

STOP WISHING, START DOING

Emma Davies

"Stop wishing, start doing."

That was the snappy little quote her mum had given her. Stuck on her fridge, Becky had read this a million times. The message had obviously got through as now she found herself at Heathrow Airport with a round-the-world ticket. Her thirty strong shoe collection had been condensed down to three and everything else had been crammed into her scratchy new backpack complete with a Union Jack badge haphazardly stitched on.

This was going to be her treat after graduating from university before she had to do some adulting and get a proper job. She was going to get out there, explore the world and meet new people. That summer her three-year relationship with her fiancé had come to an end. A gentle giant but when he'd said earlier in the year that he was ready to settle down, get married and have children, she'd picked her jaw back up off the floor and realised they were in very different places. The relationship had been easy. Safe. But did she want that?

Truth be told she would be happy with safe right now because her emotions were all over the place. One minute she was excited at the prospect of adventure, trying new things, pushing herself to the limits, the next she was terrified at the thought of venturing all around the world on her own. It all seemed so exciting just a couple of months earlier flicking through the brochures at the travel agent. That was before the planes flew into the side of the twin towers and the world seemed a much more sinister place. That was nearly the adventure over before it had even begun but she'd reasoned with herself that now, more than ever, was probably the safest time to travel.

So, when the announcement came that her flight to JFK, New York was boarding, she switched off her mobile phone and stepped off British soil for three months.

What seemed like an eternity later the impressive Manhattan skyline came into view. In no time at all, a yellow cab was whisking her into central New York and she found herself submerged in the New York underground. Everything was bigger, even the bloody Tube trains (called the subway in New York) were double deckers. She must have looked like a rabbit in the headlights.

"Do you need a hand with that?" said the American accent.

Spinning round, she found a particularly striking man smiling at her. Shocked that someone was engaging in conversation with her in the underground (you wouldn't dare engage in conversation in London for fear of someone recoiling in horror) it took her a couple of seconds to realise he was anticipating a response from her.

"Oh, um, yes, are you talking to me?"

"Yep. You there with the map upside down and now with your British accent. You look a little lost."

"That obvious, huh?" She laughed. "Yes, I could do with some help getting downtown."

"That's the same train as me and it's next. Stick with me and we'll get you there."

Not quite believing how friendly this complete stranger was being, she hopped on the subway to downtown. It turned out this striking stranger's name was Nate. He was twenty-two, had also graduated that year, and was saving up for his own travelling adventures in a month's time before he had to enter the serious world of adulthood.

The conversation flowed and when Nate asked if she'd like to join him later for a drink, she found herself giving him her number. As she exited the subway, she looked back to see Nate's smile for a second before he was whooshed into the tunnel.

"Get a grip, Becky," she mumbled to herself as she emerged into the hustle and bustle of the Big Apple.

She reminded herself that she hadn't come on this adventure to find a man. She was here for adventure. To try new things. To push herself out of her comfort zone.

New York was so 'alive'. After checking her belongings into the little hostel, she immediately went out exploring. Camera in hand, she looked ever the tourist as she snapped photos of yellow taxis, huge trucks, the New York skyline and the Statue of Liberty. Savouring the best tasting salty pretzel from a street vendor, she ambled around Central Park.

So immersed in the business the city had to offer, she almost forgot about her 'date' with Nate later. It wasn't really a date, was it? She wasn't going to see this guy ever again once her brief stop in New York was over. Perhaps this was why she'd given him her number. What's the worst that could happen? If he turned out to be a complete plonker she would be moving on to the next adventure in a matter of days, leaving Nate and the Big Apple far behind.

He'd texted her with the name of a bar not far from the Empire State building. As she approached, she glimpsed his boyish good looks and wide smile. He had a friendly face and bloody hell did he smell good as he opened the door.

"Ladies first."

Apparently, chivalry wasn't dead.

Having recently come out of a long-term relationship, Becky hadn't given meeting someone new a second thought. When you're in a long-term relationship it's easy. Routine. You know exactly what the other person likes. She should have felt nervous but actually she felt excited. Nate was so easy to talk to and had similar big dreams. The conversation flowed, so did the drinks, and looking in on this young couple you would never have known they had only just met.

"You've got to see the New York skyline at night. Would you like to go to the top of the Empire State Building?"

"Lead the way, my personal tour guide, it's on my New York 'to do' list," she laughed.

What she hadn't thought through was how they were going to get to the viewing deck 102 floors up. Becky wasn't a fan of lifts but nor did she relish the thought of climbing so many floors.

"Unless you're qualified in CPR, we're going to need to take the lift," she said reluctantly.

"You want me to lift you?" Nate asked, confused.

"What? No. Take a lift to get up to the top floor."

"Oh, an elevator," he laughed. "Don't worry, I'll be here," Nate gently replied as he took her hand in his.

A little tingle passed through her. What the bloody hell was that? Was she sixteen again?!

The lift swooped up to the top at an impressive speed. Once her stomach had caught up with the rest of her body, they stepped out onto the observation deck. The twinkling New York skyline was magical. The noise of the busy streets below muted by their height. Taxis looked like toy cars. As they walked around the observation deck, Nate pointed out places of interest. Each time he brushed against her, Becky had to remind herself that this was a one night only guide.

They talked animatedly about everything, anything. Laughed. He challenged her opinion. Teased her. They spoke about their travelling plans and all the places they were going to visit. Becky passionately spoke about her desire to travel, the next step of her adventure around the west coast of America and on to New Zealand and Australia. It turned out that Nate and his friends were starting their travels off in New Zealand.

The night wore on and, ever the gentleman, Nate

walked Becky back to her hostel. They vowed to stay in touch, and should they ever find themselves back in each other's neck of the woods they'd look each other up.

She watched Nate as he walked away down the street. He turned to offer her one last wave, a flash of that killer smile, and with that the busy street swallowed him up and he was gone. What a night! Becky had not wanted it to end. She'd never felt so alive.

But the adventure was just beginning and so she immersed herself in all New York had to offer. It literally was the city that never sleeps. Walking back from a show on Broadway at gone midnight the streets were alive with the hustle and bustle. She visited Macy's, Bloomingdale's, Fifth Avenue. Not actually buying anything, as the backpack was already bursting at the seams, but taking in all this retail heaven New York had to offer.

The Statue of Liberty, The American Museum of Natural History, Brooklyn Bridge, The Chrysler Building. So much to pack into a few days. It was fast paced, exciting, but bloody hell it was knackering.

A week later and she'd taken to the skies yet again to start her two-week Trek America trip around western America. This is what her grandad's £500 inheritance had paid for. She was sure he would have approved of her quest for adventure.

Day one orientation and Becky knew she was going to have a blast with this group of eight young like-minded thrill seekers. With supplies purchased, they all bundled into the white van with their guide Steve promising an adventure off the beaten track.

After the obligatory photos of the stars on The Hollywood Walk of Fame and the Hollywood sign, they took to the coast and made their way down to San Diego. The scenario here was in stark contrast to the jostling streets of the Big Apple just twenty-four hours beforehand. This was where the calm was going to come. Where she could finally step off the hamster wheel and just be.

Further into the trip, they passed into the Arizona desert for a stay at Betty and Rusty's cowboy camp. Becky chuckled at a sign on the outskirts that read 'Hot Beer, Lousy Food, Bad Service, Welcome, Have a nice day.' Any quibbling as to whether this was anything but authentic was burnt out around the campfire that evening. Sitting toasting marshmallows to make s'mores, Rusty regaled the adventurers with tales of the 1920s. This coming after a day of shooting tin cans out of trees, lassoing cows (albeit the fake cows) and sweating their arses off traipsing around the sweltering Arizona desert.

With the cheap beer flowing, inhibitions lowered, Becky felt the tension finally leaving as she watched the flames from the bonfire flickering up into the twinkling night sky.

That night as she lay under the twinkly stars in just a sleeping bag, she felt the most alive she had felt in her twenty-one years.

The next day, they were loaded up and back on the road heading to Monument Valley, home of the Navajo Indians. Becky and her companions gazed in awe at the vastness of the arid landscape, the backdrop to many a great western film. They watched this backdrop change as the sunset cast a myriad of oranges and reds as far as the eye could see.

Following this spectacle of colour, they were welcomed by the natives to eat with them and treated to a performance showcasing their cultural dancing. When encouraged to join in, she leapt to her feet, laughing and dancing the night away.

The whistle-stop tour of the west coast continued and it wasn't long before the little gang found themselves in the gambling capital of the world – Las Vegas.

This place was insane. There was no way they were going to be able to pack everything into the brief twenty-four hours they had here.

First stop was a bungy jump at Circus Circus. Why the hell not? Becky had been saving that for New Zealand, but the infectious buzz of this place had ignited the thrill seeker in her. She'd asked the staff to push her off if she didn't dive off after the countdown but, after only a momentary pause, she was freefalling through the air. Within seconds, her hands skimmed the cold water below before she was whooshed back up into the air just to lose her stomach (thankfully not the contents) for a second time.

Her feet weren't back on firm ground for long, though, as next up was the roller coaster on top of the Stratosphere. Certainly one way to take in the view of the Las Vegas strip. The day was spent experiencing many firsts. Playing roulette and walking away from the table a whole $20 down. Being hustled by the slots. Riding the gondolas in the Venetian. She still couldn't believe she was indoors when she looked up at the most realistically painted sky ceiling. Visiting the Coyote Ugly bar and secretly hoping Adam Garcia might put in an appearance.

After an 'All you can eat' buffet that night, the gang piled into a stretch limo. With champagne in one hand, Becky poked her head out of the sunroof and felt the wind in her hair as the limo made its way to Fremont Street for the great light show. And what a show. It was truly mesmerising. Like nothing she had seen before.

Head back, gazing awestruck at the lights dancing above, Becky was jolted back into reality with someone knocking clumsily into her.

"Hey, watch it!" And swinging around quickly: "Nate?"

All of a sudden, she wasn't going to give that big grin a piece of her mind and instead she stood there returning the grin.

"What are you doing here?"

"Last minute plans. Old Frankie here is getting married and we couldn't have him plunging into that without throwing him a bachelor party."

That night in New York they'd talked all about their travel plans, and perhaps the chance that their paths might cross in New Zealand, but this was a complete coincidence. The boys had only decided yesterday that they were coming to Las Vegas.

"Is this the English Rose you've been telling us about?" Nate's friends jested.

"Oh, so he's been talking about me has he?" Becky laughed.

"Talking about you? Hasn't stopped going on about you more like," ribbed Frank.

Was that a slight blush she saw spread across Nate's face?

"All good things I hope," said Becky as she smiled and ribbed Nate.

Quickly changing the subject, and trying to regain his composure, Nate asked what the group's plans were for that evening. Studio 54 at the MGM Grand was to be their final destination for dancing into the night. With no plans other than to drink and dance, the bachelor party from New York tagged along and the little group of travellers was suddenly doubled.

As they approached the club, Becky could hear the pulsing music and felt the thrill of the base reverberating through her body. Or was that the thrill of Nate having to get closer to her as they struggled to hear each other's animated conversation? Nate wanted to know all about her travels since they'd parted. As the evening wore on, although the group had doubled in size, they only had eyes for each other as they picked up from where they had left off in New York. Hours passed with neither of them touching their drinks. At some point Nate had swept her off her feet, quite literally, and dragged her onto the dance floor rammed with gyrating bodies pulsating away in their own hedonistic worlds. Glitter guns popped as acrobats suspended from the ceilings twirled above them at dizzying speeds.

And then the music was slowing down, the lights were coming up and she found herself looking into those chestnut brown eyes.

"Becky, you really are the most intriguing woman I've ever met," Nate said, smiling down at her and brushing away a sweaty mass of hair that had fallen across her face. "Sweat and all!"

In that moment, she wanted to close her eyes and kiss him, but what good would that do? How was she losing herself to someone she was never going to see again? She hadn't thought of herself as someone who could develop such intense feelings at first sight. Well, technically second sight, but the fact remained their paths were unlikely going to meet again.

But Nate didn't kiss her. Maybe Americans weren't as forward as the blokes back home. Maybe they were more gentlemanly. Or maybe it wasn't an American thing, and it was just a Nate thing. But the fact he didn't make the move fuelled that spark further. She found herself involuntarily moving forward and, after a short kiss on his cheek, she said, "Oh Nate, if only we didn't live an eight-hour flight apart!"

Although it had felt like time had stood still, inevitably the night was drawing to an end, the glitter needing to be swept away to rain down again tomorrow. The group was bumbling out of the club and getting ready to go their separate ways when Nate gave Becky's hand one last squeeze.

"Until the next time then, right Becks?"

"Until the next time."

With that, she sensed a strange feeling swell inside her. Bloody hell, what was that? Was she going to cry? Forcing a smile, she stepped up to plant another kiss on Nate's cheek, repeated her goodbyes and turned back to her little group. As she turned one last time, she could see the guys from New York tussling Nate's hair, mocking him, but he too shot a quick glance back and smiled that winning smile.

The following day, Becky woke with a smile, thinking about the mad shenanigans of yesterday, but the edge was tinged with a little sadness. Bloody hell. She hadn't come away looking for love. What was this? She didn't even know, but what she did know was that Nate was engaging, kind, interesting, adventurous. This was only the start of her adventures. She was going to need to remember these encounters for the fun that they were and move onto the next stage of her travels.

And the next stage was to leave the good old U S of A and head off to New Zealand. What a long flight that was but, fortunately being a night flight, and exhausted from the many stops of the past couple of weeks, she spent the majority of the flight in a peaceful slumber.

A new country brought with it new people and new experiences. Starting off in Christchurch, she couldn't wait to start her 'hop on hop off' Kiwi experience on the big green bus. Again, she was surrounded by young people of all nationalities, out there on a trip of a lifetime, searching for new adventures. And New Zealand had adventure by the bucket load.

Queenstown made you do crazy things. Again, Becky found herself bungy jumping, this time off the Kawarau Bridge. Next, she was shrieking from the thrills of white-water rafting on the Shotover. In stark contrast, Milford Sound's fiord, plush rainforests and sparkling waterfalls provided a sanctuary of calm and magic. As a fair-weather lover, a trip to the Arctic had never featured on her 'bucket list' but here in New Zealand she found herself hiking up Franz Josef Glacier complete with pickaxe. She swam with the dolphins at dawn in Kaikoura. Such beautiful contrasts in one country.

With only a few days left in New Zealand, she found herself wandering through the Abel Tasman, quite possibly the most beautiful and peaceful place she'd ever been. Her thoughts turned to Nate and how sharing this experience with him would have been the cherry on the cake. She wondered why she hadn't been able to get hold of him. She knew he was in New Zealand now, starting his own adventure. He'd excitedly texted her a couple of days ago saying he had landed on the north island and was due to hop on a small plane to the south. She hadn't needed to change any of her plans as he said he'd catch up with her in Nelson before she headed off to Australia.

Her thoughts of Nate were rudely interrupted as she stumbled on a tree root. Falling heavily onto her right ankle, the peace of the park was shattered by the piercing shriek that followed the unnatural snapping sound. Initially she was more embarrassed as her two newly made friends from France came rushing to her aid. However, from the piercing pain that followed, Becky knew something terribly wrong had happened.

Hobbling back to the ferry, supported either side, a mixture of tears of frustration and pain fell freely. Once back into Nelson, Becky had the big green bus all to herself as the tour guide drove her to the local hospital. A couple of hours later and an X-ray confirmed the tree root had done a right number on her ankle and it was broken. Fortunately, nothing requiring surgery and, as long as the swelling had gone down by the following day, fashioned with a fetching moon boot and instructions to check into a hospital in Sydney, she could be on her way. Thank goodness for insurance.

That night, as she lay in the hospital bed, unable to sleep, she couldn't help but feel a little melancholy. This wasn't part of the plan. She'd worked her arse off to pay for this trip. But then having a word with herself she reminisced over the wonderful experiences she'd already had, the many open-minded and free-spirited people she'd met. She smiled, knowing this was a little blip and that she could rest with friends in Sydney. With a bit of luck, her ankle would heal quickly, and she could continue on her travels up the east coast of Australia.

Naturally, her thoughts turned to Nate. It would have been wonderful to have met up with him one final time. To experience something together in this magical country. But then what would that have achieved? She remembered the pang of sadness from Las Vegas when they'd had to go their separate ways. Another encounter, more memories made, would only have deepened the blow when she moved on. Because these travels were all about moving forward. A once-in-a-lifetime opportunity. Maybe it was for the best that she hadn't been able to get hold of Nate.

She should remember their encounters as precious moments in time. And it was these memories that she played through again as she drifted into sleep.

Just as Becky fell into blissful unconsciousness, in another part of the hospital, another young person was gaining consciousness after two days in a medically induced coma, much to the relief of the medical team.

"What happened?" came the almost inaudible whisper as the young man struggled to talk.

"You're safe now. You were involved in a plane crash. The swelling on your brain was so great we needed to put you into a medically induced coma. You came in critically unwell, but we're encouraged with the progress you've made," the surgeon stated. "Can you remember your name?"

"Nate. My name's Nate."

★★★

Emma lives with her husband Darren, small humans Chloe and Toby and fur baby Arthur in Devon.

Lawyer by day, representing nurses, she is now an author by night!

Emma has always dreamed of writing a book. Ironically sharing her journey through breast cancer treatment gave her both the time and the subject. She self-published *Take my hair (but not my humour) One mum's journey seeing off breast cancer* in October 2020. https://amzn.to/2QuXGoJ £2 from every paperback sold is donated to FORCE cancer charity.

She was also a contributing author to *The Girls Who Refused to Quit, Volume 3* published February 2021. https://amzn.to/3vP55iP

And now she's turned her hand to a short fiction story she's definitely got the writing bug!

You can find her on Instagram, Facebook and Twitter: @lightboxblogger or www.lightboxblogger.co.uk

A WOLF IN SHEEP'S CLOTHING

Michelle Chambers

Allison awoke to the metallic taste of blood in her mouth. Her head was throbbing as if she had been out the night before, but she didn't remember even making it to the pub. As she slowly regained consciousness, she remembered getting off the phone with her boyfriend, Jake, letting him know that she was just walking up the High Street and to order her a gin. She had taken a left down the alley between Clark's and Waterstones as it was the fastest way to The Shepherds Inn. She was already running late and didn't want to continue fighting her way through the rush-hour crowds. The streetlamp could only light the first twenty metres or so of the alley and, as soon as Allison was out of the light, she instantly regretted taking the shortcut. She remembered reading about two murders that happened recently, but the police seemed to give the impression that they were unrelated one-off killings; surely she'd be safe. She swore she heard someone behind her but couldn't see anyone. She started to quicken her pace as she rummaged in her bag for her pepper spray but, before she knew it, she had been hit from behind and felt the warm blood rush from her head down her cheek before collapsing on the pavement.

She could feel her shoulder-length black hair sticking to her face, the blood acting like glue. Allison opened her eyes and instinctively tried to sweep her hair off her slender, olive face and back into place but realised she couldn't. Her arms and legs were chained to the wall and she could only move them a few centimetres. She wanted to scream but decided against it as whoever did this to her could still be there. She tried to stay calm and figure out where she was, but the more she tried to understand, the more confused she became.

Although her limbs were shackled, she was surrounded by books, candles, a huge antique-looking desk and a few windows. The windows were small and close to the ceiling, making her think that she was in a basement. She couldn't see any light or anything that would give her any clue as to where she was or if those windows shone out to the street or a garden. None of her belongings seemed to be in the room and other than a cut in her jeans and being barefoot, nothing seemed out of place, as if it were totally normal to have a woman chained to the wall. There were no bars on the windows, the door was just a normal door, gothic-looking, but she didn't sense that she was in a cellar or some really fucked up version of *Fifty Shades of Grey*.

Suddenly, Allison could hear a muffled voice that kept getting closer to the door. She went limp as if she was still unconscious as the door creaked open. The voice said 'I did, but it wasn't a play on words, although I think I like that, the "master of pieces", hmmm, it can be a working name. I have more work to get to, I look forward to talking to you more, but I think the press should be there shortly, so you'll need to get ready.' And they put the phone down.

Turning to Allison, they said, 'No point in lying limp and hurting yourself, I know you're awake.' Startled, she straightened up and opened her eyes to see the person who did this to her, trying to reconcile what a sadistic sociopath looks like in her head with how completely different the non-descript man was who stood before her. She had never seen this man before and tried to find something about him that would help identify him to the police if she ever got out alive, but there was nothing. Even as she looked him in the eyes, staring at his evil soul, it didn't feel evil, it felt as though he were a caregiver somehow, which made it even worse.

As she tried to piece together who he might have been talking to and how he knew she was awake, he said, 'Cameras. You didn't think I'd just leave you in here without making sure I could watch you? I have a lot of work to do, and can't be everywhere at once, but want to make sure you're well looked after.'

'You call this being looked after? I'm chained to the FUCKING wall!'

'No need for that, I put you in the nice room, I could have put you in the shed with the others.'

'Others?' Allison said, horrified.

'Yes, others, but you wouldn't like them, they don't

have much to say these days.' He chuckled to himself as if he'd said something funny.

Allison's eyes began to well up.

'Oh, did you think you were the only one? Oh, hunny, no. The artistic mind is always at work, I have several masterpieces on the go. Little miss Gabby just discovered my latest piece of work, let's tune in, shall we?'

Allison hadn't noticed the television on the wall as it gave the appearance of a mirror when turned off. For the old feel of the room, it seemed to be decked out with high tech equipment with the hidden cameras and flashy TV. He had turned it on to the BBC, which was live from Queen Elizabeth Park. There seemed to be a lot of journalists surrounding this one tired-looking woman. Allison watched intently as Robin Keyes said, 'DCI Brewyn, we were alerted to a horrific crime that took place here this morning, can you tell us anything about that?'

'The department will be releasing an official statement on the matter later today.'

'What about the other two murders? Do you believe that they are linked?'

Allison could tell the officer was caught off guard, but her answer didn't make the world of difference to her current situation.

'At this time, we are not prepared to give any details of open cases.'

'What about the phone call you just took, was it the killer? They said they would be calling you to see if you liked their art. Was there anything significant about the bodies that would help identify them?'

Allison looked at the man who was clearly admiring the chaos and he tapped the side of his nose and pointed to the TV.

'The killer cuts the bodies into pieces, and wants us all to see their masterpieces, and this is just the beginning.'

Allison's heart sank, now knowing her fate, looking at the man who most certainly was the devil as he smiled wickedly at her.

'Gabby didn't seem as happy as I am, but she'll come around.'

'What are you going to do me?' Allison wept.

'Now, where would the fun be, if I told you? As I said before, there are others, so you have a little bit of time left. You can reflect on your life, and how you ended up here in the first place.'

'I'm here because you knocked me out and locked me up here, I didn't just wander in!'

'Ah, the innocent victim. Well, let me tell you that none of my pieces are pure of heart. So, before you go and blame this on me, maybe you should take a long look in the mirror, Allison Keach.'

Allison was stunned; how did he know her name, she knew she didn't recognise him, but how did he know her?

'Oh, yes, Ms Keach, I know *all* about you. All creative geniuses do their research. Allison Keach, thirty-two, born on the 12th of July 1988 to Janice and George Keach in Salisbury.'

The man with dead eyes began smirking at her now as she sat there silently trying to process how someone she had never met could know so much about her. And what is all this 'creative genius' crap? This guy was a psychopath and Allison began to worry that her family was in danger now too. Her lips began to quiver, and her eyes began to well up at the thought of this.

With sincere sympathy, he went over to her and stroked her cheek. 'Aww, don't cry, I didn't mean to upset you. Trust me, I mean no harm to your family, they have done nothing wrong, and, if you're lucky, I may let you speak to them before this is all over.'

Allison recoiled at his touch and how quickly he could go from a monster to someone who cared. Her stomach churned and she could feel the vomit working its way up her oesophagus and burning the back of her throat as she was sick all down her front.

The compassionate murderer jumped back and said, 'Oh, hunny, look at you, you're a mess, let's get you cleaned up.'

Allison spat the remaining sick from her mouth onto the floor as she said, 'Get the fuck away from me, you psycho. You kidnapped me, have me chained to a wall, know all about me, yet you want to clean the sick off me? What the hell is wrong with you?'

She stared at how quickly his face turned from concern to nefarious and it scared her how the two seemed to live within this one man. His face became a deep shade of carmine that she had never seen on a person before. She could hear his heavy breathing, and his heart raced as he inched slowly closer to her face. Allison winced as his lips were mere centimetres from her ear as he said in a devious voice, 'Looks like we will start sooner rather than later.' She watched him leave the room, slamming the heavy, arched medieval door.

Shit, shit, shit, Allison thought as she began to sweat. *What is he going to do to me? What should I have done? Should I have played sweet? Oh God, is Jake looking for me, will they find me?* As she fell deeper into despair she started to scream for help, hoping someone would hear her, that someone would come.

Not only did her cries go unanswered but she didn't hear her captor walking down the corridor and opening the door. She immediately stopped her pleas for help and stared at him as his once crimson face had now returned to his unremarkable European Caucasian hue.

Still seething, he said, 'Don't stop screaming on my account, I quite like it.' He laughed. Allison's face froze as she contemplated her next plan of action, but was drawn to the conspicuous-looking box that now sat nicely on the desk. It was a little larger than your typical attaché case but smaller than a trunk, its worn brown leather caressed its edges and was adorned with faded brass combination hasps.

He manoeuvred himself between the desk and Allison, so she was now staring at his back as he proceeded to scroll his thumbs across the stiff locks, slowly and methodically turned each one into its rightful place. Allison could see the hair on the back of his neck stand with excitement as whatever was in the case was obviously a great source of enjoyment for him.

She listened intently as the hasps snapped upright, allowing the case to open. The tired hinges creaked as he lifted the top of the case to expose what lay inside. Although he covered most of her view with his broad frame, she could still see the lacklustre red velvet that lined the inside of the case. He stood there for a moment, gazing at the contents of the case, and exhaled enthusiastically.

Allison was stunned as he span around quickly but was still covering the case. 'So, little Ms Keach, as you were so inclined to be rude to me when I was only trying to help, I think it's only fair that I return the favour.' She stared into his black eyes as he continued. 'It's been a while since I've used these items, I guess I didn't consider the others worthy enough, but you, you, Ms Keach, definitely *deserve* this,' he said wickedly.

He moved behind the desk, allowing all the items to be on full display to Allison. As she gazed across them, she only noticed one knife. She wasn't sure whether to be relieved or not, but the other items looked foreign. They didn't look old enough to be antiques but were undoubtedly something that wasn't mass-produced. As she studied the contents, it hit her what they were; medieval torture devices. He must have made them himself or had them made. They were too 'new' to be from the actual Middle Ages. She remembered her history A-level course in almost full detail now, the PowerPoint from Mr Hackett's class flicking through her mind as she tried to remember the name and purpose of these heinous instruments.

He gently placed his hands on the knife, glided it out of its position and showed it to Allison proudly as if he were holding up a trophy.

'Do you know what this is?' he asked Allison as he

turned the knife slowly, which allowed the light to bounce off its smooth stainless-steel finish.

'A knife,' Allison said simply.

'Oh, no. Not just any knife, it's a flaying knife. Traditionally used to skin people alive. Fun, eh? If I were to start with this, I'd probably skin those lovely size six feet you have. Not the top, just the soles to make running away impossible.'

Allison felt the blood drain from her face at the thought of being skinned and this sicko enjoying it. She tried to speak but no words would come out.

'Oh, but don't worry, I won't start with this,' he continued. 'Now, let's see what other toys we have in here,' he said, as his whole body rippled with pleasure. He carefully placed the flaying knife back into its place as he ran his fingers across the other items.

Allison was paralysed. Not that she wanted to die, but if this was the end, she wanted it to be quick, not be tortured for some psycho's enjoyment. 'Just kill me already,' she said without conviction.

'Now, where would the fun in that be? Doing it my way will allow us to get to know each other better.'

'Know each other better? You already seem to know everything about me, and by the little I know about you, I don't want to know any more.'

'You always have a sassy comeback, don't you? I wasn't going to use this but maybe I will.' He turned around, facing the case once again, and took out what looked like a wine opener with leaves around it. As the PowerPoint was running through her mind again, it landed on the pear of anguish and she silently mouthed, 'No.'

'Oh, you recognise this, do you? The pear of anguish is an old favourite, as it can be used anywhere there is an opening.' Allison recoiled at the thought of that thing going anywhere near her.

'This one is a bit more sophisticated than the ones used in the Middle Ages, I've had it made by a very talented blacksmith. The turning mechanism now moves effortlessly. Sure, there is some resistance once the leaves start to open inside of you, but there is no need for oil or another person to help as with the original ones.'

Allison, unable to move due to the chains, knew that he could do whatever he wanted and she couldn't do anything about it. She could scream and no one would hear her, and it would give him pleasure. She felt truly powerless, defeated and just wanted all of this to be over.

'Now, the pear of anguish, as you might remember, was used on women, liars and homosexuals. For gays, it would be put into their rectum, women in their vaginas and liars in their mouths. I was thinking before that I might use this on you because of your sins, fornication, which led to an abortion, but since you have a sharp tongue, I may use it on your mouth…' He paused. '… Or both,' he said with delight.

He cradled the torture device as if it were a newborn baby. He walked closer to Allison with devilish intent. Next to where she was chained up was a bookcase and, as he scrolled his long thin fingers across the titles, he landed on one and pulled it. Suddenly, the wall Allison was strapped to began to move. She began to move backwards, slowly opening up to an all-white, very sterile room. The table stopped moving when she lay horizontal, with each half of her in each room. When everything shifted, there was space on either side of her for her tormentor to move freely around her.

He began to take the pear of anguish and run it along her slender legs up to her pelvic area and let it rest there for a moment until moving it up her torso and in between her breasts. He proceeded to drag it upwards towards her face. He twirled it across her chin and, as he began to lay it upon her lips, Allison could see the wonderment that consumed his whole being.

'Well, let's get you cleaned up, shall we?' he said nonchalantly. 'We will have to get you out of these dirty whore clothes first,' he said as he started to unbutton her low-rise Levis.

Allison interrupted, 'If you're going to torture me, I'd at least like to know the name of the person responsible.'

'Well, I personally feel this is your own doing, but seeing as you won't make it out alive, I don't see any reason why I couldn't oblige. I see myself as a cross between H.H. Holmes and Francis Bacon. Gabby and I were just working on a name, maybe the "master of pieces", which has many connotations in this line of work, but to you, you can call me Urbain Grandier.'

★★★

Michelle is a four time #1 bestselling author based in Leicestershire. She is originally from Chicago and met her husband whilst getting her Masters' Degree. She has two kids, two dogs and is enjoying living in the East Midlands. She is a Mindset Coach and Mentor and has her own business The Best You. The first lockdown in the UK also led her to crochet, which transpired to an absolute love for the art and another business, OH my Design.

www.thebestyouinstruction.com
www.facebook.com/ohmydesign.crochet

CHRISTMAS 2020 – A VERY SHORT STORY

Georgia Johnson

As I was to decorate my own real tree for the first time since coming to live in Bungay, I decided to set to the task of getting it home from the florist's early.

The tree was a seven-foot blue spruce, luckily encased in a net wrap, which meant getting it home was feasible albeit cumbersome.

I struggled up and down the gentle inclines of the quiet small market town where I lived, hauling my precious prickly possession – or my furry friend, as I had quickly dubbed it – to its vendor, who looked at me quizzically as I declared that there was 'no time like the present' and that I was quite capable of lugging the unwieldy edifice back with me.

'You need…' her voice trailed off.

'Someone gallant?' I queried. 'Well, when they said a good man is hard to find they weren't wrong.' I flounced out with the sort of panache that would put the heroine of a screwball comedy to shame.

'Happy decorating!' she called out hopefully after me.

'Surely it is worth it if only for the comedy value,' I mused, clasping the really rather heavy seasonal offering under my camel-coated arm. I was very glad I had some gloves with me and had put them on, even though the sleety snow that mizzled down soon soaked them along with my damp package, which had been left to fend for itself with the others out of doors; all the better that its needles should not fall off before it had even started.

The rough prickles of the evergreen hurt as I hauled my purchase along, but I felt warm, and it was actually pleasantly bracing to be carting a Christmas tree around a market town in early December. I was glad, though, that I was still young, unlikely to succumb to a heart attack on this day as a result of my optimistic exertions, nor too many pitying looks as I was well dressed and suitably clad for the occasion.

Once I had returned *chez moi*, I marvelled at the fact I had not snapped off the tree's pointy tip and that all I had to do was to find some sort of star or even angel to crown the whole thing off once I had managed to actually fix it in its stand and erect it. Still, the fact remained, that a woman, not yet fifty, living alone with only a Christmas tree for company, was on some level de facto pitiable if not pitiful over the season of goodwill. I decided not to entertain this maudlin train of thought for a second longer; if other people didn't get my sense of humour that was too bad.

Some days had passed since the transportation of Picea Abies to my flat and now, as night enveloped the rural

Suffolk enclave, it stood proudly in the corner of my living room. As it was, my sense of humour had pretty much kept the whole of my previous life afloat, but some aspects of life just aren't a laughing matter, even though gallows humour does and will always have its place.

I had managed to shock a number of people with delicate sensibilities who were incredulous at my a) having got the giant tree home, and b) having paid tens of pounds for it. At present, there seemed to be no subsidence of the evergreen, even though it was a foot over tolerance and the ornaments I had arranged tastefully on it twinkled gently in the glare of the electric light. I rejected tinsel and so-called fairy lights and so the tree seemed to take on a magical presence of its own, buxom one contact called it.

Mysterious dark green tree, I would have said – whether it was male or female seemed a moot point, as it had been decidedly hacked from its roots and was most definitely for ornamental purposes only. The waft of pine oil was comforting and reminded me of Christmases long past where I still believed in Santa and the magic of his journey across the sky with reindeer and his sleigh. The cavernous centre of the tree seemed inviting, the dark depths of it more tranquil and still than dark and foreboding, no matter how short the days now were as we waited for the equinox and the coming of the King – not Elvis.

My arrival in Suffolk had coincided with tales of not long redundant sites of execution on dreary crossroads where the rain seeped into the fertile country soil through the pockmarked tarmac. My Christmas tree was a shining specimen of Victorian progress and optimism in a part of the world where time almost seemed to be suspended and modernity was merely a flash in the pan in a landscape that stood tired and cold, groaning again for spring, which always came, no matter what fads and fancies manifested themselves on the glittering surface.

A tradition that manifested itself over a century a go seemed newfangled in these parts, and the ever-pressing distraction of festivity and festiveness, pointlessly although gloriously frivolous, as I gazed admiringly at my creation alone. Only the gentle blip of the computer reminded me that I was not utterly cast adrift on a hopeless wave of Christmas nostalgia – entirely of my own doing, of course.

My gallows humour had served me in good stead, especially last Christmas when Hugh told me he was leaving, and I wondered out loud if he was Father Christmas. What possesses a person, not yet thirty-five, that they must leave the country to be in the desert with a Bedouin tribe, I still couldn't work out. Yes the rat race is gruelling, yes we all wonder if there is more to life – don't we? However, not many pack their bags on Christmas Eve to take a flight to Cairo. Still, Hugh was definitely a one-off. I assumed he was having the time of his life as the Instagram pictures definitely seemed to suggest so.

Again, my mobile phone blinked at me. I had elected to turn off all notifications as I didn't really want to be assailed by each and every photo opportunity on Hugh's travels. Still, I couldn't help myself and peered down at the glossy screen. I was rather surprised by what I saw.

Instead of the usual plethora of adverts for handbags and other luxury goods that were a hang over from my time living in London, I was staring straight into the face of an individual who I immediately recognised. It was myself, but an image of myself I had never seen before. To say I was disconcerted would be putting it mildly. How, I immediately wondered, had this image come to be available on the internet and, more perplexingly, who had taken the image?

Now the one other thing that is true of myself, aside from the fact that only I would see the comedy in being abandoned on Christmas Eve, I never like to let a mystery get the better of me; therefore, sighting myself in the cyber ether but most decidedly from another era was an event I was never going to let get the better of me. Who had obtained access to my mother's hard drive, in other words…

I know the octogenarian was becoming increasingly senile, but she could still manage to bank remotely and only needed occasional assistance with her online supermarket shop, so the probability that she was a victim of a cyber scam was almost as shocking as Hugh's announcement had been. Whatever next, I mused to myself. Not wanting to worry the woman, I elected not to fire off a text to her and instead began to mull the probable origins of my very own Wikileak.

★★★

Having won a county cash prize for her creative writing in her teens, it seemed as if Ellis Johnson was always destined to be an author.

This is her first attempt at 'romance' writing as Georgia Johnson. She is very grateful for the guidance of Jen Parker and her team at Fuzzy Flamingo for assisting her in taking it forward.

According to The Masterclass series on short story writing, short stories can be just as powerful and moving as longer worlds of fiction and a short story is like using a flashlight to illuminate a hidden corner. If her work resonates with anyone on any level she shall be very pleased and shall also consider the Masterclass subscription money well spent.

The Mendham Writers helped Writer Johnson along the way, Ron French, Sheila Preston et al as well as the illustrious Ian Nettleton, Bridport Prize winner, at the National Centre for Writing.

You can find out more here:
http://www.byellisjohnson.com

SHADOWS OF THE NIGHT

J A Simones

★★★Please note that this is a sample of, Shadow Of
The Night, a novel written by J A Simones, also
known as Alexandra Simones. The full version will
be available later this year.★★★

1975

A few simple, easy to follow, step-by-step instructions.
Place tie around neck, cross the wider end over the thin
end, run the wider end under the tie and pull across once
more, then pull wide end through the centre, loop through
the knot and tighten, and *Voila*. It's as simple as that. Or so
Walter thought when he had made his first ever attempt at
tying his own tie on.

It was the eighteenth day of December. The day of Walter's
sweet sixteen. A day that he and his friends had been
planning for almost a year. The day his life would really

261

start to take a turn for the better, or so he thought.

At 8am he was supposed to get ready and meet Ronny and Lucas at the bus stop. They would sneak onto the number 276 bus through the back doors whilst Chanelle distracted the driver as she frantically searched for her bus ticket. Once safely onboard, Ronny would signal with a slight nod of the head, and Chanelle would be given permission to board the bus on the condition she ensured she'd have her ticket with her the next time. This, of course, the norm, as Ben, the driver, enjoyed the cleavage that she would put on display. Most of the time this was for his pleasure solely as she enjoyed his wandering eyes over her curves, but on the odd occasion, she was prone to flaunt elsewhere. Given that Ben was ten years her senior, she knew he would know better than to complain, as their affair had to be kept a secret. Expressing his anger would only arouse suspicion. She was the only one from their group of friends that came from a wealthy background, therefore she had a reputation to upkeep for the sake of the family. She was expected to be, "little Miss Perfect". Some days she thought that their friendship only survived because of freebies, but she soon put that thought to the back of her mind after Walt had rescued her in the middle of the night when a date had gone wrong. Something neither of them ever speak of, but it had formed the backbone of their friendship.

The group of four would travel silently to Canning Town where they would be met by Tamz, Marcus and Sam, the remaining three of their tribe. Once together, they would buy a dozen cheeseburgers from McDonald's before roaming the town. Whilst the girls pondered through shops and chatted in secret, the boys would flick pennies, comparing whose would reach the furthest. The loser would then be the one to track down someone stupid enough to buy them some cheap wine or cider. Once this was achieved, although this was not always the case, they would hide in the abandoned warehouse that stood like a shadow toward the far end of town. There, they would stay until dark. Because no party could happen before then. No party was an *actual party* until the hustle and bustle of the busy city started to fade into the night and its bright lights replaced the day's natural rays once the city had gone home to sleep. Only then could they blast the music from their wind-up radio whilst the boys rolled joints and the girls danced fiercely without a care in the world, their arms gently moving like butterflies that spread their wings for the first time. A sight that arose the boys each time.

But this day was not to be. The only celebrations he would engage in would be those of the wake as he gathered with his distant family to celebrate his father's fond memories. Instead of standing here, in front of his father, who should have been the one to teach him the knack of tying a tie for the first time, he was alone. His hands were trembling with fear of being exposed for what he truly had become. Frail and weak, afraid of his own shadow as he attempted once again to complete the impossible.

'Come here, darling. Let me help.' His mum took his hand and ushered him to the hallway where its bright light would help her tired eyes see more clearly. Mrs Grey knew her son liked his independence. His brother would ask for help with most things, including pouring milk over his cereal for breakfast. His hands had always been less sturdy compared to Walter, and she supposed it was one reason he thrived in his own company and independence. Accepting help was not part of his nature since he was a giver. She had meant well and loved him dearly. 'I know this is a tough day for you, son. But we will get through this. I promise.' Her smile was kind, her eyes glimmering from the tears that had fallen from them. She turned her face towards the ground, busying herself with his tie and examining the untied laces of his freshly polished shoes.

'You don't have to hide them, Mum,' Walt said. He knew all too well that his mum was somewhat of an expert at hiding her emotions from him, well so she thought. But deep down he could feel her pain. He could see into her soul. Feel what she felt. See what she saw. Their bond had been strong since the day he had been conceived. They had both been convinced of that. Even more so over recent years.

Her eyes met his, but for a moment, all fell silent. 'I have cried all morning,' she admitted as she pulled the tie tight. 'I don't think I have any more left to shed.' Her smile was faint but sincere.

As Walt reached out to his mum and held her close in his arms, he wondered what their future would hold now that they were alone. What would their destination look like and how would they get there? He was only sixteen and still had so much more to learn. But he felt confident, now more so than ever, that he would be willing and able to be the man of the house and take care of his family. And he was even more certain that he would do a better job than his father ever did.

Tammy gently approached mother and son from the side entrance of their flat, which could be accessed via the main entrance, but her preferred method was to hop over the barrier that led to the balcony door. Her footsteps gave her away before she had even appeared. Her usual sneakers had been replaced by her sister's four-inch heels, and although it took her a lot of strength and effort to walk in a straight line without a fall, her appearance did not give this away, for she carried herself well. Better than most women.

"Are you both ready?" Tammy asked. The question was silly, she knew that, but what else should you say when someone has died? Is there such a thing as the right things to say?

Walter reached for her hand and pulled her in. Not only was she his best friend or the one he had loved most of his life, but she was like family.

"Come on," Walter's mum said, "let's do this."

2021

The rattling had woken Tammy at the crack of dawn. It had woken Walt too, but he played dead for another hour thereafter, hoping to sleep away the pain, wishing he could simply drift into the unknown. But with every breath of air that gushed against the building and its delicate frame, another creak could be heard as it settled into the structure from floor to ceiling. That is where it would seek permanent residence. It was nothing more than a thin sheet of glass that kept the storm from entering their home. What was once a portal of light only days ago was now the barrier that threatened to cave in.

The oversized bed seemed insignificant as it stood alone in the centre of the room. It was there that he would lie every morning like a body in a casket, simply waiting for death to claim him. Walter took a deep breath, for he knew that at this hour he could no longer close his eyes. Any minute now the kettle would awaken, its whistle carrying through the empty corridor that ran along the outer wall of their ground-floor apartment. It would reach his room within four seconds, and that was his time. That is when he would lift his lifeless body from its slumber. Not for the love of freshly brewed tea, nor for the undying love he had for his wife of twenty years, but simply for the desperation of peace and solidarity within his mind that would ignite his soul like wildfire for only a few moments of his life. Those were the ones he cherished dearly.

The hairs on the nape of his neck stood fiercely every morning, like clockwork. This was his daily reminder that his time had come. Walter knew all too well what would happen if he didn't close the doors in time. The risk of being caught was simply too risky. If he looked for even a second longer or a little too deep into those piercing red eyes, the flame would ignite, the heat would soar straight through him and it would be too late. No one would be safe. Once the lid flipped, there would be no closing it without a fight. All control would be lost. The thought made him shudder. So, at 6am sharp, he would float along the corridor like a bird of prey. His palms now held pools of sweat. A secret like this would ruin a man's life. Everything he had worked for over the decades, he had served to this life, his wife. Everything. Snapped away from under his feet like a rug that grew wings and no longer saw a need for him.

All temptation was lost moons ago, for he had learnt his lessons the hard way. Staying in the shadows was safest. And so that is where he would leave him until death came and took what was rightfully his. The shadow would remain its home, its safe place. At arm's reach. This was safest. For everyone.

If you've enjoyed what you've read, please do leave us a review on Amazon.

If you'd like to know more about Fuzzy Flamingo's publishing services then go to the website: www.fuzzyflamingo.co.uk

Find us on Instagram: https://www.instagram.com/fuzzyflamingodesign/

Or Facebook: https://www.facebook.com/FuzzyFlamingoDesign

If you are a book lover, whether you're a reader, a writer, or both, join our community: https://www.facebook.com/groups/ fuzzyflamingobooklovers

Printed in Great Britain
by Amazon

61134031R00160